D0049146

PAM MUÑOZ RYAN

Becoming
Naomi
León

SCHOLASTIC PRESS

NEW YORK

W

Library of Congress Cataloging-in-Publication Data

Ryan, Pam Muñoz.
Becoming Naomi León / Pam Muñoz Ryan. — 1st ed.
p. cm.
Summary: When Naomi's absent mother resurfaces to claim her,
Naomi runs away to Mexico with her great-grandmother and
younger brother in search of her father.
ISBN 0-439-26969-5 (hardcover)
[1. Great-grandmothers — Fiction. 2. Brothers and sisters — Fiction.
3. Family problems — Fiction. 4. Mexican Americans — Fiction.
5. Mexico — Fiction.] I. Title.
PZ7.R9553Be 2004
[Fic] — dc22   2004000346
12 11 10 9 8 7 6 5 4 3   04 05 06 07

Printed in the United States of America   23
First edition, September 2004
The display type was set in Dalliance Roman.
The text type was set in Perpetua.
Book design by Marijka Kostiw

to Jim, Annie, Matt, Tyler,

Marcy, and Jason

thank you

Tracy Mack,

Leslie Budnick,

Marijka Kostiw,

and Joe Cepeda

a table of contents

a rabble of yesterdays

*I always thought the biggest problem in my life was my name,
Naomi Soledad León Outlaw, but little did I know that it was the
least of my troubles, or that someday I would live up to it.*

*It had been a double month of Sundays since Gram, Owen, and
I were knitted together snug as a new mitten. I can point a stick,
though, at the exact evening we started to unravel, at the precise
moment when I felt like that dog in an old Saturday morning car-
toon. The one where the mutt wears a big wooly sweater and a fox
runs up and pulls a hanging-down piece of yarn. Then the fox
races off with it, undoing the tidy stitches one by one. Pretty soon
the poor dog is bare to its skin, shivering, and all that had kept it
warm is nothing more than a bedraggled string.*

1 a paddling of ducks

There we were, minding our lives with the same obedience as a clock ticking. A few weeks earlier the sun had switched to its winter bedtime, so even though it was early evening, the sky was dark as pine pitch. That meant that Gram, Owen, and I couldn't sit outside on the white rock patio. Instead we had to crowd around the drop-down table in the living room/kitchen of Baby Beluga. That was what Gram called our Airstream trailer. She was the absolute expert at calling things what they resembled and thought it looked like a miniature whale next to all the double-wides at Avocado Acres Trailer Rancho.

The trailer park was called this because it was surrounded on three sides by the largest avocado ranch in Lemon Tree, California. The name Lemon Tree did not appeal to Gram's sense of description because, as she pointed out, there wasn't a stick of citrus in sight. A giant plastic lemon did sit on a pedestal at the Spray 'n Play, a combination car wash-deli-playground and one of our favorite places. That lemon was a tribute to the fact that there used to be fruit orchards in San Diego County, before the builders came and put a house on every scratch of spare dirt. Except for the avocado grove, which was smack in the middle of town and the last countrified land in Lemon Tree.

We had already put away the dinner dishes from Wednesday chicken bake and Owen started racing through his second-grade homework like a horse on a tear. People were usually fooled by his looks and thought he was low in school due to being born with his head tilted to one side and scrunched down next to his shoulder. It had straightened a little after three surgeries at Children's Hospital, but he still talked with a permanent frog voice because of something inside being pinched. One of his legs was shorter than the other so he walked like a rocking horse, but other than that, he was just fine. Contrary to people's first opinions, he got the best grades in his class.

Gram, in her usual polyester pantsuit and running shoes, was doing her weekly hair set, rolling what little blue hair she had on those new bristle curlers that require no hairpins. (I was not being mean about her hair. It really looked blue in the sunlight.) And I mulled over my sorry situation at school, which was three boys in my fifth-grade class who had decided that Outlaw was the funniest last name in the universe. They did not give me an ounce of peace.

"Have you robbed any banks lately?" was one of their favorite sayings, along with jumping out at me, throwing their arms in the air, and yelling, "Is this a stickup?"

My teacher, Ms. Morimoto, said to ignore them, but I had tried and it did no good. I was fed up, so I was making a list of what I could say back to them that might be embarrassing. I wrote across the top of my notebook page, "How to Get Boys to Stop Making Fun of My Name."

I scooted my book in front of Gram to see if she had any ideas.

"Naomi, I have lived with that name since I married your great-grandpa, rest his soul, almost fifty years ago, and I am due proud. Besides, there are worse things in life."

"But you don't go to Buena Vista Elementary," I said.

She laughed. "That's true, but I can tell you that boys have not changed an iota and they are hard to humble. You know my true feelings on the subject. How about writing, 'Those boys *will not* bother me'?"

Gram said that when you thought positive, you could make things happen, and when it *did* happen, it was called a self-prophecy. If you wanted to be the best speller in the class, you said to yourself over and over, "I *am* the best speller in the class," and then before you knew it, you were practicing and becoming it. It was sort of like magic, and Gram believed it to her bones. But it didn't always work the way I hoped. At one time Owen and I were the only children in the trailer park. I thought positive every day for a month for more kids at Avocado Acres but all that moved in was a family with a teenager and a brand-new baby. Gram insisted my positive thinking had succeeded, but I had been greatly disappointed.

Before I could write down Gram's suggestion, Owen

sneezed, and it was a big one, the kind that sprinkled spittle and left his eyes all teary.

"Owen, you got it on my page!" I said, smoothing my paper, which only smeared the wet spots.

"Sorry," he said, and then he sneezed again.

"Company's comin' twice," said Gram, matter-of-fact. It was another of her Oklahoma notions, and she had a million of them that she believed whole heart. This one being if a body sneezed, someone would pay a visit.

"We already know for sure that Fabiola's coming over," said Owen.

Fabiola Morales lived with her husband Bernardo, just a stone's throw away in the middle of the avocado grove. Bernardo took care of the three hundred trees, and in return he didn't have to pay rent on their tiny house. Fabiola and Gram were newly retired from Walker Gordon department store, where they had worked for thirty-five years as seamstresses, doing alterations with their sewing tables face-to-face. If that wasn't enough familiarity,

Fabiola came over every night, Monday through Friday, to watch *Wheel of Fortune*. So far, Gram and Fabiola had watched 743 during-the-week episodes without missing once. It was their claim to fame.

"Well then, Fabiola counts for one," said Gram, patting a curler in place. "I wonder who'll be the other?"

I looked at Owen and rolled my eyes. A fly zooming in would fulfill Gram's prediction.

"Maybe Mrs. Maloney?" said Owen.

Mrs. Maloney was eighty-eight and lived in the double-wide next door. She came out every afternoon to water her cactuses, rocks, and cement bunnies, and only then did she ever come over for a visit. Gram said we could count on Mrs. Maloney for two things in life: one was wearing the same pink-checked cotton robe every day (I suspected she had a dozen hanging in her closet), and the other was going to bed at six in the evening.

"Nope, it won't be Mrs. Maloney," I said. "It's past six."

Chewing on the end of my pencil, I got back to my list, which Gram said was one of the things I did best. I had all kinds of lists in my notebook, the shortest being "Things I Am Good At" which consisted of 1) Soap carving, 2) Worrying, and 3) Making lists.

There was my "Regular and Everyday Worries" list, which included 1) Gram was going to die because she was old, 2) Owen would never be right, 3) I will forget something if I don't make a list, 4) I will lose my lists, and 5) Abominations. I made lists of splendid words, types of rocks, books I read, and unusual names. Not to mention the lists I had copied, including "Baby Animal Names," "Breeds of Horses," and my current favorite, "Animal Groups from *The Complete and Unabridged Animal Kingdom with over 200 Photographs.*"

Mr. Marble, the librarian and the absolute best person at Buena Vista Elementary, gave me the book yesterday when I walked into the library at lunchtime. He said, "Naomi Outlaw (he always calls me both names), today is your lucky day. I have a treasure for you and I've already checked it out on your card. I give this to you with a flourish." Then he scooped the book into his palms, knelt down on one knee, and held it out to me as if it was a box of jewels. (I added *flourish* to my "Splendid Words" list.)

Mr. Marble allowed me and two other students to eat lunch at one of the oval library tables every day. It was breaking school rules to eat there, but Mr. Marble didn't mind. He just smiled at us, straightened his bow tie, and said, "Welcome to the sanctuary." (*Sanctuary* also went straight to "Splendid Words.") John Lee was one of the library lunch students. His parents owned Lemon Tree Donuts. He was the roundest boy at Buena Vista Elementary, and one of the nicest. The other was Mimi Messmaker. (Her name was on my "Unusual Names" list, along with Delaney Pickle, Brian Bearbrother, and Phoebe Lively.) Mimi didn't hang out with all the other girls in our grade either, the ones who were always comparing makeup and going to sleepovers. She was nobody special at school, just like me, but she didn't know it. She had no use for me and once whispered, "trailer trash" when I walked by. After that I never said a word to her, and that suited us both.

"Naomi," said Gram, "is there a page in your notebook titled 'Ways to Annoy My Gram'? Because if there is, I'd appreciate it if you'd add your unruly bangs to that list."

I quickly reached up and corralled a triangle of hair hanging in my eyes. I was trying to let my hair grow all one length, but in order to keep my bangs pinned back I needed three clips on each side. Gram had taken to calling me "brown shaggy dog" because of my wild mop and my predisposition to brown-ness (eyes, hair, and skin). I took after the Mexican side of the family, or so I'd been told, and even though Owen was my full-blooded brother, he took after the Oklahoma lot. He did have brown eyes like me, but with fair skin and blond hair in a bowl haircut that Gram called a Dutch boy. Due to my coloring, Owen called me the center of a peanut butter sandwich between two pieces of white bread, meaning him and Gram.

"Thank you for making your old granny happy," said Gram, tucking a stray lock of hair behind my ear.

"You're not *that* old," I said.

She laughed. "Naomi, I am your *great*-grandma and according to most folks, I had no business raising you and Owen. Those who carried gossip said I had one foot in the grave and should've known better, but I took you on like spring cleaning anyhow. The joke was on everyone else because I got the prizes. That was my lucky day when I got you two."

Owen looked up from his binder. "Today's *my* lucky day. Guess what's one of my spelling words? *Bicycle!*"

Any coincidence in Owen's life, such as wanting a new bicycle and having the word show up on his spelling list, made him feel lucky. Whistling, he started writing *bicycle* over and over on a piece of paper.

Gram finished rolling her hair, leaving lines of white scalp staring at us.

"My clown head is on," she announced.

Owen and I never argued with that description because the yellow and purple curlers did give that effect. Gram clicked the television remote to find the tail end of the nightly news. I closed my notebook, giving up for now on my list and knowing full well I wouldn't be able to say boo to those boys anyway. I reached into the built-in cabinet above my head and pulled out the plastic salad bowl holding my latest soap carving.

When Owen and I first came to live with Gram, I had slipped into being silent and my hands shook all the time. I was too young to remember what caused it all, but Gram's practical solution was to keep my mind and hands busy. Soap carving had been Bernardo's idea, and he said I was born to it. He would work in his shed doing his hobby, making wood boxes and little miniature bookshelves, then painting them every bright color with scenes of little towns and sunsets. It was art from his city, Oaxaca, far away in Mexico. And I would sit next to him with a bar of soap and a carving tool. Gram was nervous to death about me using a knife, so Bernardo started me out with a bent paper clip. As I proved my worth, I graduated to a plastic knife, a butter knife, and finally, a paring knife.

I picked up the partially carved duck and my knife from the pile of slippery shavings in the bottom of the bowl. I had already finished two other ducks, each a little smaller than the other, but I wanted a third for the shelf above the kitchen sink. I was never content to carve one of anything, preferring at least two or three for a companion-ship of lions or a circle of bears. I pulled the knife across the bar of Nature's Pure White. The soap sloughed off easy into the bowl, looking like shredded white cheese. I scraped in an arc, finishing off the curve of the back and up to the tail. The dry film on my hands felt like a thin glove, and every few minutes I put my palms up to my nose to take a whiff of a smell that reminded me of being a baby.

"Done with spelling!" said Owen, closing his books. He came over and stood next to me, watching. "Naomi, how do you know what to carve?"

"I imagine what's inside and take away what I don't need," I said, not looking up. Slowly, I added the finishing touches on the duckling, scratching out the appearance of feathers with the pointy end of the knife. I loved this part of carving, the etching and the grooves that made the figure look true to life. I was getting ready to level the bottom, so it would sit flat and not wobble on the shelf, but I didn't get one more pull of the blade before someone knocked on our door.

The knocking became a pounding and someone yelled, "Anyone home?"

"That's not Fabiola," said Gram. "Naomi, you expecting anyone?"

I shook my head. I thought I'd heard that voice before, but I couldn't put it to a face. Setting the bowl aside, my hand twitched and I missed the counter. The three soap carvings tumbled to the floor in a rain of white feathery shavings.

"For heaven's sake, Naomi," said Gram. "It looks like a fox got into the henhouse. Clean that up lickety-split and I'll get the door."

Gram got up, turned off the television, and reached the door in one step. "Did I mention that company's coming twice? I hope it isn't someone trying to sell me something and me in my clown head! I surely don't need door-to-door makeup."

If it was a salesperson, they'd have to talk to Gram

through the screen because she never, ever set foot outside the trailer in her hair curlers.

Gram opened the door. She narrowed her eyes like she was trying to focus real hard.

While I cleaned up the soap mess, I craned my neck to see who was standing on the step.

"Well, aren't you going to invite me in?"

Gram truly looked like she'd seen an apparition, which is what she calls a ghost. She finally stepped aside and a lady walked in, pulling a big black plastic garbage bag that she had to tug through the small door opening.

"I got my belongings to fit in this one bag and that's a miracle," said the lady. "You all were hard to find. I looked in three phone books before I found the address. I never suspected you'd be living in a trailer park!"

She wore jeans, red boots, a black leather jacket, and a hefty splash of sweet gardenia perfume. Her hair looked like that crayon called maroon, the one that's not purple and not red but something in between, and for some reason I couldn't take my eyes off her lipstick. It was the exact same color as her hair and went up and down in a perfect rounded *M* on her top lip.

Owen sniffed the sweet air.

The lady looked at Owen and me and said in a singsong way, "Hi-eee."

When she got no more than a blink from us, she sat down on the covered bench that served as the seat for the kitchen table. When the table was put up, the seat doubled as a foldout bed. She took a long look at us, then turned to Gram, who was still holding the door wide open, and said, "Just look at these babies!"

All I could think was that nobody in their right mind would ever mistake me for a baby. Sure, Owen looked more like a kindergartner than a second grader, but it was for positive that he was nowhere near babyhood.

Gram finally shut the door.

The lady said, "My, you two have gotten big."

A strange, queasy feeling crawled around my stomach.

"Naomi? Owen?" she said. "Get yourselves on over here and give me a hug!"

Slowly Gram shook her head back and forth, still looking dazed. "You can't just waltz in here after all these years
and expect these children to recognize you."

"Don't be silly," said the lady. "Children always know
their mother. Don't you, darlings?"

The words swarmed in my mind.

"Our mother?" said Owen, his gravelly voice cracking.

My heart pounded so hard that I feared it would
leap across the room, and my thoughts started jumping
up and down on a trampoline and bouncing off the corners of my mind. Her face was round like Owen's and
her skin was so white it was almost pink, like Owen's.
I supposed that came from all the Oklahoma in her, but
she didn't look anything like the pictures of the blond
teenager that Gram had shown us over the years. Still,
her eyes and the smell of her perfume were strangely
familiar.

Gram said, "Naomi. Owen. Go on in your room so I
can talk to Terri Lynn."

"Oh, that's not my name anymore. I changed it. To

Skyla. Isn't it beautiful? Naomi and Owen, come on over here. I would like to hug my children."

We looked at Gram and she nodded.

Owen went first and reached out to hug Skyla, but before he could, she said, "Oh, look. You have something stuck to your shirt," and she reached down and started to pull off the long piece of tape pressed across his chest.

Owen clasped his hands over the tape.

Gram and I yelled at the same time, "No!"

"He . . . he likes it," I said.

"It's just a little comfort thing he does," said Gram.

Some kids had blankets or stuffed animals they dragged around. Others got contentment from twirling their hair or sucking their thumbs. Owen had to have tape stuck to his shirt — the clear kind people used to wrap presents. For some reason it brought him a peculiar satisfaction.

Skyla pulled her hand back. "He wears it on purpose?" She looked from Gram to me to Owen. Then she started laughing. "Woman, what have you done to this boy?"

Gram's eyes got all beady, like pigeon eyes. "He's just fine. There's no harm done."

Owen looked at Skyla as if she was a fairy princess, but still didn't take his hands off the tape. He gave her his biggest jack-o'-lantern smile (I swore his mouth was too big for his face) and said in a dreamy sort of way, "It's all right. You didn't know."

I walked over to Skyla and she put her hands on my shoulders, keeping me at arm's length. She did that sort of leaning-in type of hug, with a quick cheek-to-cheek touch. It was not the I-haven't-seen-you-in-seven-years type of hug that I would have expected. Then she did the same to Owen. I put my arm around Mr. Starry Eyes and herded him to the bedroom.

As soon as we were there, Owen grabbed my hands and started jumping up and down. "It's our mother! It's our mother! Maybe she missed us and wants to know all about us and has presents for us —"

"Shhh. Owen, stop!" I said. We were only a lick and a promise from the living room/kitchen, separated by a flimsy accordion door, which I did not shut. I wanted to hear the conversation word for word.

"I need a place to hang out for a while," said Skyla.

"These children don't know you."

"Well, it's about time they did."

"You should have thought of that years ago," said Gram. "I'm not going to have you coming in here, Terri Lynn, and messing with their lives."

"I told you, my name is Skyla."

"And where did that come from?" said Gram.

"My new boyfriend, Clive. He said I didn't look like a Terri Lynn. He said I look beautiful, like the sky. I'm Skyla Jones now. I went back to my maiden name. And for your information, I'm not here to mess up these kids' lives. I'm just here for a visit while Clive's at training."

"Training?" said Gram.

"He's a tattoo artist," said Skyla. "And don't look at me with that hard-eyed stare. There's good money in tattoos. He's learning dragons and flames from a guy in downtown San Diego. Clive is staying with him at the studio and it's too small for me, too, so I thought since I was in the area, it would be a good time to, you know, reconnect with my children."

"Where have you been all this time?" asked Gram.

"I've had some trouble. . . ."

"What kind of trouble?" said Gram.

Even though my ear was straining to catch a phrase, their voices gathered in a whorl of whispers I couldn't hear.

Then we heard Skyla yell, "You can go along with me or not. I'm their mother and Clive says I have rights."

Now we could hear Gram loud and clear. "You left those children with me when that boy was a year old and covered head to hide with infected insect bites. Naomi was four and didn't even talk until she was almost six —"

"Don't make out like it was such a big deal," interrupted Skyla. "Naomi was always stubborn and quiet, and Owen just had a few fleabites."

"No, ma'am," said Gram. "Naomi went to a counselor for two years. She had selective mutism — that's what it's called — from insecurities and Lord knows what other trauma during her young life. That's what the counselor told us, and Naomi still doesn't talk much. Owen was on antibiotics for three months to get him cleared up. There's no telling what went on in Mexico that caused those children's abominations. And now, seven years later, after you never sent a card or made a telephone call to even let us know you were alive, you want to talk about your rights?" There was a little hitch in Gram's voice. "Terri Lynn, they . . . they're tied to me. You promised I could raise them proper with no interference. That's what we agreed on before you left."

"Naomi and Owen seem fine now, so I couldn't have been *that* bad. And I've changed my mind about seeing them, that's all. Now, I'm going to meet Clive but I'll be back later. And I'd *appreciate* you calling me Skyla."

When the trailer door closed, the floor jiggled beneath our feet. Owen and I ran to the louvered window and looked out. There was just enough brightness from the porch light to see Skyla get into a red Mustang, touch up her lipstick, and pull away from the trailer. She tore out of the trailer park going faster than the posted fifteen-mile-per-hour speed limit.

Part of me couldn't wait to see her again. The other part of me was wringing my hands like a contestant in the Worrywart Olympics. All of a sudden I had a million questions. Why did she come back? How long was she going to stay? Would she like us? Would we like her? My thoughts dived into a jumble in the middle of my mind, wrestled around until they were wadded into a fisted knot, and attached themselves to my brain like a burr matted in a long-haired dog.

3 a lamentation of swans

Dripping wet, Gram didn't weigh a hundred pounds, and even wearing her running shoes she didn't reach five feet tall. Now, sitting down with her skinny neck drooping over the table, she looked like a swan peering into a lake.

Owen and I slid in across from her. She folded her hands and looked at us. Her face seemed tired, but not happy-tired like after working in the garden all day with Fabiola. Instead, it was worry-tired I saw in her eyes, as if something bad was about to happen. The purple and yellow curlers on her head seemed much too cheerful for her face.

"I know you probably don't remember much about your mother," said Gram, talking real slow as if we wouldn't understand her if she sped up. "I've told you the story of how Terri Lynn came to live with me. . . ."

We had heard it, but only once in glorified detail because Gram was not one for rehashing events from the past. Owen and I had retold it to each other so many times that we might as well have been reciting from a storybook. It had started way back, after Gram was widowed. Her daughter got married and ran off to live in Kentucky. Gram said it broke her heart to lose her only child to folks in a state so far away. Her daughter and son-in-law had one child, Terri Lynn. Gram had only seen her a few times during her young life. Then, when Terri Lynn was a teenager, her parents suffered a car crash and died two weeks later in the hospital. Terri Lynn was sent to live with her other grandparents. From what Gram could figure out, Terri Lynn defied them so much that they finally didn't want her anymore. Gram was her only other living relative, so they put Terri Lynn on a bus to Lemon Tree. She arrived mad at the world and almost grown.

"When she came to live with me, there just wasn't much I could do with her, wild as she was," said Gram. "And then . . . and then . . ."

"Then Walker Gordon had their summer company

picnic and you brought Skyla," I continued. "And Fabiola and Bernardo brought some men who were visiting them from their town in Mexico."

Gram nodded. "Terri Lynn met Santiago, a gentle, sweet man, and so handsome. He looked like those Latin singers you see in magazines. He was smart and full of life and spoke English enough to get by. Those two loved each other like crazy. For a while at least. They were really just children themselves."

"Then they got married," said Owen. "Then they had Naomi. Then they had me."

"They lived in a little studio apartment, but it was like putting a pack of angry cats in a wood box," said Gram, shaking her head. "The obligations of you two came into the stew, and their marriage just never thickened. They thought that if they went to Mexico, everything would be better."

"Then they took us to Rosarito Beach so our dad could make lots of money fishing and our mom could make lots of money braiding people's hair on the beach," said Owen.

"Then they got a divorce and our dad stayed in Mexico and our mom went to find her life and we came to live with you."

"My apartment was small as a cracker tin," said Gram. "And here I was with you two and Owen a whirling dervish. My notion was that children needed wide-open space to be wild monkeys. Fabiola told me about the trailer rancho and how it backed up to all the avocado trees. I suspected that Fabiola and Bernardo wanted us close so they could help out with you kids. They always felt kin to you, being that your dad was from their town. And well, I thought it would be good for you to be around them and exposed to your Mexico side."

"You filled in real nice," I said, patting Gram's hand.

"And now our mother is back," said Owen, looking confused. "That's a *good* thing, right?"

"Owen honey, it's the good and the bad I'm worried about," said Gram.

One of her favorite sayings was that the good and the bad of any situation were sometimes the same. When I was younger I had trouble holding my brain on that thought, but now it was starting to make sense. I even had a list in my notebook called "Things That Were the Good and the Bad All Rolled into One": 1) We had a trailer so we lived real simple without a lot of stuff, 2) We had avocados growing nearby and could eat as many as we wanted to the point of getting sick, 3) Gram was an expert seamstress and made all of our clothes out of polyester-blend remnants, and 4) Gram was retired and could devote her every waking moment to me and Owen.

Now I would have to add: 5) Our mother came back. What did Gram suspect the bad would be?

"Where is she going to sleep?" asked Owen. "How 'bout she sleeps in my bed and I could sleep on the floor? I can pretend I'm camping."

Baby Beluga had a living room/kitchen, Owen's and my bedroom with two side-by-side captain's beds (with drawers underneath), a short hall that ran right into Gram's bedroom, and a tiny bathroom. That was it.

"I think we're awful close to camping already," said Gram. "She can sleep on the foldout under the table."

"Where did she go?" said Owen.

"Out." Gram frowned.

"Maybe she'll be right back," said Owen, his voice excited. "Maybe she just went out to pick up a pizza and ice cream so we can sit around together and talk about what we've been doing for all these years."

Gram and I looked at him. His never-ending good nature was grating on me.

"Owen," said Gram. "I give you more credit than that."

We heard a quick double-knock on the door, then it opened.

"*¡Hola!* Hello, I am here. I made tapioca." It was Fabiola, just in time for *Wheel of Fortune*. She held a ceramic bowl and wore one of those flowered bib aprons that went over her head, but she was so short and round that the apron was rolled up at the waist so it wouldn't drag on the floor. Gram said Fabiola's mission in life was to feed the world with a smile. Her face was set with lots of little smile wrinkles next to her eyes and framed with brown permanent-waved curls. And I had never once seen her without her little gold dot earrings.

Fabiola took one look at Gram's face and asked, "What has happened, María?" Mary was Gram's given name but Fabiola always called her the Spanish version.

"Terri Lynn was here. She's come back."

"But we're not supposed to call her Terri Lynn," said Owen, "'cause she changed her name to Skyla, after the sky."

"Skyla?" said Fabiola, her forehead wrinkling.

No one said a word. I could hear water trickling from one of the neighbors' garden hoses.

In just a few seconds Fabiola's face changed to worry-tired, too.

"Come," said Fabiola, setting the tapioca on the table. "We must tell Bernardo."

Gram got up and put on her sweater. Then she handed Owen and me our sweatshirts.

I looked at Owen. His eyes grew big and his mouth dropped open. He slid off the bench, opened the drawer, took out a roll of tape, and studied it. Then he stuffed the whole thing in his pocket.

I picked up my notebook, took Owen's hand, and followed Gram and Fabiola out the door.

That was the instant I knew with conviction that Skyla walking through the doorway of Baby Beluga was life-changing serious. I knew it for two reasons, and I suspected Owen knew it, too. First, Gram had marched outside the trailer and was following Fabiola into the avocado grove still wearing her clown head. Second, and what locked the possibility of catastrophe in my mind, was that Gram and Fabiola were going to miss *Wheel of Fortune,* and *that* was going to mess up their 744 nights-in-a-row record.

A floodlight cast a path of brightness straight through the avocado grove. Not that we needed it. Over the years we had worn a foot trail to Fabiola's front door and could get there blindfolded. Up ahead the glow lit up the yard like a bright island, and the tree branches seemed like giant black umbrellas over our heads. We passed the chickens, who made gentle clucking sounds as we walked by their makeshift wire coop. Normally we'd stop to pet them, but Gram and Fabiola had a purpose to their walk that said no stopping. They led us into the little clearing toward the flat-roofed house.

Lulu, Fabiola's miniature poodle, ran toward us yapping, her bobbed tail wagging back and forth and her black curls shimmying with excitement. Owen picked her up.

Bernardo came out of his work shed and stood in the square of light from the doorway, holding a piece of sandpaper and a short plank of wood. He was barely taller than a fence post with skin the color of toasted almonds.

When he first saw us hurrying toward him, he tipped his straw cowboy hat back on his gray-haired head and smiled wide, not even minding that he was showing us his crooked teeth, some of them pointing sideways.

"*¿Qué pasó?* What happened?" he asked, his smile fading.

Fabiola spoke in Spanish, the words racing off her tongue. She ended the string of sentences by putting her hands on her hips and saying, "Skyla."

A body would think that since I was half Mexican I could speak the language, too, but I couldn't. I understood a little just from being around Bernardo and Fabiola all these years, but whenever I tried to copy them, the words felt like marbles moving around in my mouth.

Bernardo looked suspiciously around the yard, as if someone might be watching us, and said, "We should go inside."

Fabiola and Bernardo's small house was wide-open spacious compared to our trailer. It had three bedrooms, one of them set up as a full-on sewing room where Gram and Fabiola still did alterations. Currently they were working every day on a bride's gown and fourteen bridesmaid dresses for a wedding coming up the first weekend in December.

In the living room, striped crocheted blankets rested on the back of the couch and chairs. Colorful braided rugs made little bridges from one room to another, and Bernardo's bookshelves hung on every wall. Photographs of their two sons from high school graduations and in their United States Navy uniforms crowded the end tables, along with school pictures of Owen and me.

Without saying a word, we all sat in our spots in the living room: Bernardo in the recliner with Owen on his knee, Fabiola on one corner of the couch and me on the other, with Lulu wriggling between us, and Gram in the straight-back rocker.

I opened my notebook and waited.

Gram said, "Naomi, I'm not sure taking notes is in order."

"Just in case," I whispered. I didn't want to forget anything important that might be said.

Gram took a deep breath. "I always worried this day might come."

"What's going to happen?" I asked, my voice barely a breath.

"I'm not sure," said Gram. "I suppose she has a right to visit you and you have a right to get to know her. More than that, I want her to see that you kids are healthy and happy and dug-in deep here with me. I hope I can remember to call her Skyla. I just don't want to get her riled."

"The children? She could take them?" asked Fabiola.

"When she showed up on my doorstep seven years ago," said Gram, "I didn't know if they'd be with me for a few weeks or a few months. I knew enough to have Skyla write out a letter giving me permission to get them doctors and medicine, if they needed, and to enroll them in school and such. But other than that, I don't have claim to them . . . except that I raised them. After so many years of her being absent, I added my last name to Owen's and Naomi's on all their records and papers so we'd have a frame for a family. That was just my fancy and not legal-like."

Before that our names had been Owen Soledad León and Naomi Soledad León. When Gram tagged on her last name, Outlaw, I took it in stride (until this year), since it made her so happy.

"She has had a very difficult life," said Fabiola. "Maybe she is growing up now and wants to present herself to Naomi and Owen, and that is why she is here."

I thought Fabiola leaned toward Owen's disposition when it came to looking on the bright side of everything.

"I would sorely like to believe she's changed," said Gram.

"Changed?" I said.

"Naomi, she was always as temperamental as a bead of water on a hot skillet. I am hoping she has settled some."

"You want the children to stay here, with us?" asked Bernardo.

Gram didn't answer right away. "No, better we're together." She took a deep breath and stood up. "I should get them in bed and make up the foldout."

Fabiola stood up and gave Gram a big hug. Gram's eyes watered up.

Fabiola hugged me and Owen, too. Then Bernardo walked us all the way to the edge of the grove.

Gram swiped at her eyes in the dark of the trees. I had never once seen Gram cry from sadness and was not accustomed to seeing her unsettled by her emotions. My insides wobbled as if I was standing on a three-story roof looking down.

After I was in bed, I closed my eyes but couldn't sleep. I tried as hard as I could to remember something about my mother. Memories from a place far away in my mind struggled to get to the front of my brain, but they swam in slow motion, stroking through thick syrup toward my clear thinking spot. All that surfaced was my past imaginings of what she might be like.

Over the years, the top three on my preferred list of "Possible Moms" were 1) Volunteer, 2) Business, and

3) Nursery. I had pretended she was one of those smiling moms who came to school twice a week, volunteered in class, and helped with yard duty. She invited my friends over after school and was president of the Parent/Teacher group, and all the teachers fought over me every year because they knew if they got me in their class, they would get my wonderful mom, too. Sometimes I imagined a business mom who wore suits, fancy scarves, diamond earrings, and high heels that clickety-clicked down the halls. She would visit my class on career day and talk about her important job in a big office in San Diego. I even thought she might be like some of the moms who worked in the plant nursery nearby. She'd wait on the corner to walk Owen and me home from school every afternoon, wearing a green-stained apron and holding a bouquet of flowers.

But right off the mark, Skyla didn't match my list or fit the pictures in my mind.

I did have one recollection of my father and Mexico. Owen and I were huddled in a room near the ocean. I could hear thunder and lightning and waves crashing. It was raining so hard that the roof leaked, and when I looked up through the sprinkles of water I saw a swirl of color — a bobbing, dangling dance of pink and blue and yellow above my head. What could that have been? A dream? I remembered Owen pointing to the ceiling and laughing in that way he had, like a batter of coughing and giggling. I rocked him, afraid to move off the bed. I cried and cried until our father rushed in.

He swooped us up into his arms and took us to an old church where people had gathered, seeking safety from the storm. We were in a basement, cots set up in rows, and women serving soup. I remembered crying into my father's flannel shirt, which tasted salty. To get my mind off the thunder and lightning, he found a bar of soap and carved an elephant. He gave it to me, and I fell asleep clutching it. When I woke up, he was gone and never came back. Bernardo always said my talent for carving must have passed from my father's hands to mine. I would have rather had my father.

I pried the rest of the story out of Gram when I got older. She explained that our father had been out on a fishing trip and our mother was supposed to be watching us. She had taken off though, on a shopping trip to Tijuana and left us alone to baby-sit ourselves in the motel room. Then the storm hit. Nobody could find our mother for days. She finally showed up at the church a week later, packed us up, and took us back to Lemon Tree. She told Gram that she couldn't handle two kids by herself, especially with one of them deformed. A few days later she was gone, too.

I squirmed in bed, trying to get comfortable, but my mind was still a jumble. I finally got up and pulled a box from the drawer under my bed. I opened it and carefully dug through my soap carvings of turtles, dogs, and reptiles, and pulled out a family of elephants. I arranged them on the built-in shelf above my bed, all in a line, trunks to tails. Then I put my head down on my pillow and closed my eyes, the caravan of milky statues guarding my dreams.

5   a charm of hummingbirds

In the morning I tiptoed into the living room/kitchen. Skyla rested peaceful on the foldout, her hair making a splash of almost-purple on the pillow. Without makeup, she looked younger than last night. Lying on one side with her legs pulled up a bit, the curve of her body made an empty space, like a little nest in the middle of the bed. I wished she was awake and we didn't have to go to school. I had visions of Owen, my mom, and me all huddled up together, giggling and telling stories.

I stared at Skyla for so long that I didn't notice Owen standing at my side until he nudged me and handed over a box of cereal.

Through the small, slatted window, I saw Gram watering the bird-of-paradise plants that grew on the side of the trailer. We fixed our bowls as quiet as we could and went outside to sit on the patio couch under the trailer awning.

Gram came around and sat opposite us in the two-person swing.

"Was she stirring?" Gram nodded toward Baby Beluga.

"She's sleeping," said Owen.

Gram cleared her throat like she was going to make an announcement. "When Skyla came in late last night, we had a heart-to-heart. She has assured me that she just wants to spend a little time with you. I am going to give her the benefit of the doubt and see how she behaves. I think that's the right thing to do. Besides, you both must be natural curious about your mother."

I set down my cereal bowl and walked over to Gram and hugged her hard and didn't let go.

"Don't you worry, Naomi," said Gram, patting my back. "We're going to weather this. Let's just plant plenty of sunshine in our brains."

I squeezed my eyes shut. I planted the image of me showing Skyla my carvings, one by one, and her fussing over my talent while I shined, proud as punch.

Mrs. Maloney tapped on her bedroom window, breaking my concentration. She waved at us, then pointed at Owen.

"I almost forgot," said Gram, looking at Owen. "Mrs. Maloney needs help moving her hummingbird feeder. She loves watching them through the window, with all their flitting and shimmering, but they've taken to diving and pecking at Tom Cat. I told her you'd be over after school."

Owen nodded to Mrs. Maloney and waved back to her.

"Will Skyla be here for dinner?" I asked.

"I don't know her plans, Naomi," said Gram. "But I'll make a point of inviting her."

That evening we were almost finished eating Thursday pork chops when we heard Skyla's car pull onto the gravel. A minute later she burst into the living room/kitchen with her hands full of shopping bags.

Gram, Owen, and I froze with our forks in midair, just like one of those commercials on television.

"Hi, everybody. I've been shopping! Naomi, get over here and see what I bought you!"

Skyla dropped the bags and began pulling clothes from them. "Oh, this one's for me. But here, this one's for you. What do you think of this cute top? And these jeans are perfect. I hope they fit." She held them out to me.

I had been wearing Gram's homemade clothes and the ones from the Second Time Around Shop for so long that I couldn't believe someone was handing me a brand-new pair of store-bought jeans.

Skyla looked at me and said, "Well? Are you going to just sit there? Come back to the bedroom with me and try these on."

Gram's eyebrows peaked with surprise.

I hurried to the bedroom and tried on the jeans.

"They *are* perfect!" said Skyla. "Now, try on this top. If it fits, I'm going to buy you a few more."

The light-pink stretchy top had little rhinestones in a butterfly pattern on the front. I had seen one in the window of Walker Gordon, but I never dreamed I'd have one of my own.

I walked out to show Gram and Owen. Skyla followed me.

Gram had her back to us, standing at the sink.

Skyla cleared her throat and said, "And here she is, star of screen and television!"

Gram turned around and smiled and clapped her wet hands together. "Why, don't you look spiffy! And Owen?" Gram said, as if signaling Skyla not to forget him.

"Oh, today was shopping-for-the-girls day. Next time I go, I'll shop for Owen."

Owen grinned at Skyla and said a little too loud in his raspy voice, "Thank you!"

"Is there something you've been wanting?" asked Skyla.

Owen ran to his room and came back with a magazine picture of a bicycle and held it up to Skyla. "Naomi and me love to go to Dan's Bike Shop and look at new bikes," he said.

"Owen," said Gram. "I'm not sure that's in the price range Skyla had in mind."

Skyla nodded at Owen. "Well, that's something to

think about. Now, Naomi, why don't you let me do something with your hair."

"It's a troublesome mess," said Gram. "I'd love to see it off her face."

Skyla laughed. "I have French-braided the wildest heads you've ever seen. Sit down and let me get started. Are you tender headed?"

"No," I said, pulling out the half-dozen clips and situating myself cross-legged in front of her.

As Skyla brushed out my tangles, I couldn't help thinking over and over that my mother's hands were on my head. She took a fine-tooth comb and pulled it through my hair until there wasn't the tiniest knot anywhere. Then she started at the center top, bringing up tiny strands of hair, one over the other. Her fingers were nimble and gentle. It felt as though she was playing the piano on my head. The little finger kept reaching lower and lower, carving out sections to braid into the rest.

In a matter of minutes she said, "All done and don't

you look pretty. Here, take this hand mirror so you can see the back."

I jumped up and ran into the bathroom. There wasn't one strand of hair out of place, and the braid was woven like the rolled edge of a basket.

I patted and admired it for fifteen minutes straight.

Skyla came in and stood behind me and looked in the mirror. "Naomi, you have a perfect heart-shaped face. Did you ever notice that?"

I had *not* ever noticed, but now that my hair was pulled back tight, I could see that she was right.

"Now, stay with me while I freshen my makeup. Clive and I are going out, and I want to look perfect."

I watched her put on the base and the blush and liner and eye shadow, which took over half an hour. She gave me some clear lip gloss called Wet As A Whistle. I put it on, then took it to my room and put it in my backpack. I couldn't wait to put it on at school in front of the other girls.

Back in Gram's bedroom I watched Skyla squeeze into her jeans and boots, then gather her purse and jacket.

"How do I look?" she asked, smiling.

"Nice." I nodded, the braid tickling my neck. Then I followed her into the living room/kitchen.

"Where's Owen?" said Skyla. "I have something to tell both of you."

"He's trying to coax Mrs. Maloney's cat out from under her trailer," said Gram. "Poor old Tom is scared to poke his head out for fear of a hummingbird attack."

"Well, that's neighborly sweet. Naomi, I'll tell you and you can pass it along. I saw on the fridge that your teacher conferences are a week from today. Next Thursday, right? I am planning on being there with Gram to see your school and meet your teachers. Isn't that great? I am looking forward to it. I've got to run on to Clive's right now but I'll see you all later. Bye."

After she shut the door, I could still smell her gardenia perfume.

I sat down next to Gram. She patted my knee and

looked me up and down once more. Smiling and shaking her head like she was trying to figure out a puzzle, she said, "It's real nice that Skyla wants to go to your conferences. What do you think about me staying home, just this once, so she can have some special time with you kids?"

"Okay," I said. "I could show her my clay sculpture in the art room."

Gram kissed me on the forehead. "Your hair looks pretty as a picture. Are you going to wear your new 'do' to school tomorrow?"

I quickly nodded and wondered if anyone would notice the difference.

6 ⁓ a school of fish

The minute I walked into the classroom, Ms. Morimoto said, "Naomi! Your hair looks lovely like that!"

I smiled at her and walked to my seat.

Ms. Morimoto was a Japanese version of Fabiola. She had the same exact curly hair, and instead of long aprons, she preferred flowing skirts in bright colors. Students at Buena Vista Elementary prayed to get assigned to Ms. Morimoto for fifth grade, because every year in January she took the whole class out to dinner at a fancy restaurant and to a play at the Old Globe Theatre in San Diego. It was her claim to fame. Besides that, she was nice and didn't take any nonsense from the troublemakers.

One of the boys from the back of the room yelled, "Ooooo, Naomi!"

The boys all laughed, but the girls didn't, and I could see they were inspecting me top to bottom. Sensing their stares, I sat down right away and busied myself with looking in my desk until the start bell rang. I was secretly smiling, but I sure wished I could control the warmth crawling up my neck and cheeks.

Ms. Morimoto clapped her hands to get our attention.

"People" — she always called us people — "I'd like you to meet a new student who has just transferred to Buena Vista. Blanca Paloma. She comes to us from Atascadero, California. Please make her feel welcome. Blanca . . ." Ms. Morimoto looked toward the side of the classroom.

A skinny girl with long black hair, even curlier than Fabiola's or Ms. Morimoto's, stood up and quickly sat back down.

Maybe it was my French braid, or maybe Blanca didn't know yet that I wasn't one of the makeup-sleepover girls, but at morning recess she came right up to me and started chattering away. I didn't understand two words she said.

"I don't speak Spanish," I finally told her.

Like a light flicking from off to on, she changed to English. "You're not Mexican? Funny, you look Mexican. We just moved here, you know. My mom works for ValueCity.

Know what my name means in English? White dove. What's your name?"

"Naomi Outlaw."

"Wow, you talk so soft. Get closer so I can hear you better. Just Naomi Outlaw? No middle name?"

I took a step closer and gave her the full version. "Naomi Soledad León Outlaw. But I just go by Naomi Outlaw."

"León. That means lion. You're Naomi the Lion." She wasn't making fun, just saying it matter-of-fact.

"What's Soledad mean?" I asked.

"Soledad is some big saint in Mexico. Men and women are named after her. I have an Uncle Soledad who raises goats. They stink."

I laughed.

"Who did your hair like that? It looks amazing."

"My mother," I said, the words sounding as strange as Spanish on my tongue.

"My mom never learned French braiding because she works all the time. I go to the Y for the before- and after-school programs. It's just her and me because she's divorced from my dad. We've lived in Walnut Creek, Riverside, Atascadero, and now Lemon Tree, all in two years. She's moving up in the company. So, is it just you and your mom, too?"

"I live with my gram and my brother, but right now my mom is visiting."

"Just visiting? How come she doesn't live with you?"

"She . . . she . . . left us with my gram when we were little."

"What about your dad?" asked Blanca.

"Divorced."

"Same as me. I don't see my dad very much. What's yours like?"

"I don't know. He lives in Mexico. He's never come to see us."

"You don't know anything about him? You should ask, that's what my mom always says. Ask lots of questions and you'll get lots of answers. You deserve to know about your own life. Right?"

"You don't know my gram. She's doesn't like to dig up old bones."

"That's funny. Dig up old bones. Hey, I heard we're having conferences next week. Maybe our moms could meet? Then they could arrange for us to get together. What do you think?"

"Maybe," I said. Should I tell Blanca I had only known Skyla for two days?

"Have you ever been to Mexico?" asked Blanca. "In my whole life I've never been. My dad promised he'd take me someday. Hey, did you know I get a discount on anything at ValueCity since my mom's a manager?"

Gram would call Blanca a jabber-mouth, but I liked her and was already hoping she would stick close to me all day.

I didn't have to worry. At lunch she grabbed her bag and stayed on my elbow until we reached the library.

Mr. Marble looked at me and said, "And who is this person with the elaborately plaited hair?" Then he bowed to Blanca. "Ah, the new student. I heard about you in the staff room this morning. Welcome to our safe haven. Is there a particular subject you are interested in, Blanca, because if so, I can highly recommend a book on just about anything. After all, I am a librarian. Since it's lunchtime, can I interest you in some mind food? Or, since we have an aquarium, I could also offer you some fish food."

We both giggled and sat down at a table.

"Wow. You eat in here?" said Blanca. "Like a club, huh?"

I had never thought of it that way. I just thought it was where all the leftover kids ate.

While we took out our sandwiches, Mr. Marble arranged the glass display case. First he stacked a bunch of little boxes inside and covered them with a giant silky red scarf. Then he placed dolls dressed in costumes from different countries on the little boxes.

"These are Ms. Domínguez's private collection. Ms. Domínguez in case you don't know, Blanca, is our principal. She collected these as a girl. Now, everyone close your eyes. I am going to add some ambience."

We closed our eyes.

"Ta-dah! What do you think?" he said.

When we opened our eyes, he had turned on the light inside the display case. The light reflecting against the scarves made the dolls shine with a rosy glow.

I nodded my approval.

Mr. Marble changed the case every few weeks, and he always decorated it perfect so a student just couldn't resist stopping and looking inside. Sometimes, if Mr. Marble knew that a student or a teacher had a collection of some kind, like rocks or baseball cards, he would display them. My dream was to make it to the glass case at the library and to be known for something other than my current reputation as the weird kid's sister with the funny last name, who wore clothes that matched her great-grandma's polyester wardrobe.

Blanca was right about asking lots of questions. In that one lunch period, she found out that Mimi Messmaker was going on a cruise over winter vacation and that John Lee sometimes loaded the donut-making machine. She also discovered that Mr. Marble was from Kalamazoo,

Michigan. (*Kalamazoo* was going to the "Splendid Words" list and "Unusual Names.")

When the bell rang, they all walked out ahead of me, but I hung back. Mr. Marble must have taken Blanca's cue about asking questions because he said, "Naomi Outlaw, is there something on your mind? Can I help you?"

I nodded and whispered, "My mother came back."

Mr. Marble put his hand on his cheek. "What an interesting turn of events. And how is that working out?"

I thought about that for a moment, chewing on my bottom lip. I finally answered, "I don't know. Good, I think."

"Thank you for sharing with me, Naomi Outlaw. I know how hard it is to open up sometimes. I hope you will have more to tell me later."

I nodded and gave him a little smile. I hoped so, too.

At Buena Vista we only had bus service in the mornings, so when school was out Blanca and I stood on the front steps, waiting to get picked up. I had warned her about Owen.

When he arrived with his tape and his funny walk and his throaty voice, she shrugged her shoulders and said, "That's it? You should meet my cousin. He's in junior high and he's lots weirder than Owen."

Gram pulled up to the curb in her green Toyota.

"I'll meet you right here Monday morning, okay, Naomi the Lion?" said Blanca, pointing to the steps.

"Okay," I said, waving. I had already decided I was going to add *Atascadero* to my "Splendid Words" list. As I walked toward Gram's car, I smoothed my new jeans, readjusted my stretchy shirt, and found myself smiling and feeling like a shiny penny. My new look had brought me good luck, and I had my mother to thank.

7   an unkindness of ravens

Skyla licked her fingers clean and took another piece of Wednesday chicken bake.

"Gram," she said. "One of the things I have missed, besides my children, of course, is your home cooking."

Gram sat up straighter and smiled.

"Oh, and I just remembered, I have a little surprise, and since tomorrow is the teachers' conferences and we're all together, I'd like to show it off." Skyla went to the bedroom and came back with a flurry of shopping bags. The minute Owen saw them, he stopped eating and his eyes brightened.

Skyla reached into one of the bags and pulled out a baby blue scoopneck top.

"Naomi, this is for you. And look," she said, reaching into the other bag. "I found one in my size that matches it exactly. Mother/daughter tops! We can wear them tomorrow for your conference. And . . ." She stuck her hand back in the bag. "I found raven brown hair color. I thought our hair should match, too. I'm going to color mine tonight. Isn't that wonderful?"

"I thought ravens were black," said Owen.

"The idea is that the hair color is a black/brown, Owen," said Skyla. "We girls understand that, right, Naomi?"

I pretended I knew and nodded.

Owen put his head back down over his chicken.

Over the past week, Skyla had bought me hair clips for the bottom of my braid, a pair of fuzzy tiger-striped slippers, a new backpack, a glittery key chain, press-on earrings, and press-on nails (Gram said I could not wear them to school). She bought Clive some black T-shirts, a baseball cap, and a ring with an amber stone. Even though Gram insisted there was no need, Skyla bought her a round plastic table with four chairs for the white rock patio. She announced that all the gifts were really from Clive because he gave her the money, and wasn't that sweet? But still nothing for Owen.

Before leaving the table, I nudged Owen's shoulder

and asked if he wanted to play checkers. He loved checkers, and usually I didn't offer because I hadn't won a game against him in years. But tonight he just shook his head, so I took the top to my room and laid it out on the end of my bed.

Tomorrow, my conference would be before Owen's and right after Blanca's. We'd arranged to introduce our mothers between the two meetings. I was determined that everything should go as planned. I'd be extra quiet in the morning so Skyla could sleep a little longer. (She did not like to wake up early!) I'd wear the clothes she bought me, and I'd let her braid my hair the way she liked. Hopefully, everything would be perfect, like a jigsaw puzzle where every piece was in place.

The next morning before breakfast, still lying in our beds, Owen and I whispered our plan for showing Skyla around Buena Vista.

"Owen, after my conference you take Skyla to your class to meet your teacher."

"Yeah, then I'll show her my papers that are on the bulletin board. The A papers and my science potato. It's growing real good," said Owen.

"Then I'll meet you in the art room," I said. "Then we'll take her to the library and I'll show her my reading journals and she can meet Mr. Marble."

We stayed in bed as long as possible.

When Skyla woke up, she didn't look rested. Her eyes were all red, and while she braided my hair, her hands quivered so much she kept having to start over. I smelled something like sour milk on her nightgown.

"Naomi, sit still! I want you to look pretty for today!" She gave my hair a tight jerk.

What was making her act so mean? I sat as still as a rock, hoping her mood would change.

"Now, remember, when we're at school this afternoon, just call me Skyla Jones. You know how I feel about my name."

Owen and I knew the reasons: 1) We weren't allowed

to call her Terri Lynn because it wasn't pretty, 2) We weren't allowed to call her Mom because it made her feel old, 3) We weren't allowed to use the last name León because that part of her life was said and done, and 4) Skyla Jones had a nice ring to it.

"Where's the comb, Naomi? Are you sitting on it? Move so I can find it. Owen, pick up all my shoes and put them away. This place is a mess. And after you do that, bring me a diet soda."

Just then Gram walked in. She began picking up Skyla's magazines that were strewn on the floor and the trash from her beauty makeover last night. (I was still getting used to raven brown, which made her skin look as white as mashed potatoes.)

"I'll be sewing all day at Fabiola's," said Gram, "but after your meetings you might suggest stopping at you-know-where on your way home."

Owen grinned and nodded.

"Where's that?" asked Skyla.

"Our favorite place," said Owen. "We'll show you."

"We best leave for the bus stop in a few minutes, so hurry out of your pajamas," said Gram.

I dressed in my baby blue top and jeans.

When Skyla saw me she squealed, "Naomi, we are going to look like twins!"

I blew out a breath. Everything seemed to be getting back on track.

By the time I gathered my homework and books and stuffed my lunch sack into my backpack, Owen appeared wearing navy dress slacks that Gram had made him two years ago. They still fit everywhere but the length, riding high waters above his ankles. He also sported the matching polyester vest, a long-sleeved white shirt, and a tie. My heart skipped a little beat when I saw him. He had increased his tape usage considerable.

Gram managed a smile and said, "Owen, you look very handsome this morning. Your teacher will probably give you extra credit for showing up looking so dapper, right, Skyla?"

Skyla looked Owen up and down. "Well, yes, I suppose so, but Owen, don't you think if you took off all that ridiculous tape, it would make a better impression?"

Owen shrugged his shoulders and gave her a lopsided smile.

"Well, I'll see you all later," said Skyla. "I'll be there at two-fifteen on the button to meet your little friend and her mother, Naomi. Then we'll go to your conferences."

Gram herded us out the door. I knew Owen's going-to-a-wedding outfit was going to make for some hoots and whistles on the bus.

I was right, and it didn't stop there. As soon as we got to school, Dustin Mullholler, one of the boys who taunted me about my name, walked up to us.

"Hey! It's the Outlaws and one looks like a *Mexican bandido*. Steal anything lately?"

I wanted to tell him to leave us alone, but as much as I tried I couldn't say a word.

"What's this, Outlaw Boy? Oh, you robbed the office store." He yanked the tape from Owen's chest, strip by strip. When the last piece was peeled off, Owen dropped to the ground and started to shake and spit. A straggle of kids crowded around. Dustin panicked and frantically searched to see if a teacher was watching. He picked up the tossed-about pieces of tape and pressed them back on Owen's shirt. "Hey, kid, I didn't mean it. Here's your tape, kid. Get up before the teacher sees you lying there. Get up, kid."

With the tape back in place, Owen opened his eyes, got up, brushed himself off, and walked away, his suit dirty from the playground.

"Retard!" yelled Dustin.

Everyone laughed.

I just stood there watching the whole thing like it was a movie. Why couldn't I speak up and defend Owen or myself?

Finally I ran to catch up with Owen, the flush of embarrassment still on my cheeks. Owen smiled so big that all his teeth showed, as if the joke was on everybody else. Didn't he even *know* the joke was on him?

He took one look at my strained face and said, "I fell down on purpose, Naomi."

"Why would you do that? It just makes everything worse!"

"They didn't mean it," he said. "They were just teasing."

Why did he always have to look on the good side of everything? "Owen, don't you care what people think about you?" I said. "Kids will like you better if you don't . . . you know . . . do crazy things. Skyla would probably like you better, too, if you tried to please her."

I immediately wanted to take my words back. But before I could say anything, Owen spied a penny on the walkway and ran to get it.

"Hey, Naomi. 'Find a penny and pick it up, and all the day you'll have good luck'!" He held up the penny. "I found a penny and our mother came back and she's coming to our conferences today." Owen looked at me with big cow eyes and said, "I think that's very lucky."

I melted inside and, for an instant, I felt lucky for

something, but I didn't know what. I messed up his hair. "Yeah, Owen, that's lucky all right."

He pulled one of his tape strips off his chest and pressed it to my backpack. I knew full well that he'd run after me if I didn't accept it.

That afternoon Owen and I stood on the steps of Buena Vista Elementary with Blanca and her mother during the fifteen-minute break between our conferences.

Mrs. Paloma wore her red ValueCity smock and kept glancing at her watch.

"My mom has to go back to work pretty soon," said Blanca. "She has a meeting."

"Skyla will be here," I said, searching the street for the red Mustang.

"Yeah, she's coming for sure," said Owen. He had already wandered down the steps several times to look up and down the block.

Parents and students who had the next appointments

hurried into the building, and those who were finished walked toward their cars.

"Naomi, I would really like to meet your mother," said Mrs. Paloma. "But doesn't your conference start at two-thirty? It's that now."

"She'll probably be here any second," I said, my stomach sinking.

The comings and goings settled down. I heard the school buzzer inside the building, which meant the next session was starting. Owen kicked a little rock around in a circle. I kept my eyes on the street. Blanca reached over and took my hand.

I couldn't look at her. "She said she was coming."

Mrs. Paloma said, "I'm sorry, Naomi. We'll have to do this another time. Come on, Blanca, I'll drop you off at the Y."

Blanca followed her mother. Halfway down the steps, she turned around, put her hands out, and shrugged, as if to ask, "What happened?"

It was almost five o'clock when Ms. Morimoto found us, still waiting. She took us inside to the school office, where Ms. Domínguez called Gram. "There's no answer at the home number," she said to Ms. Morimoto. Then she looked at Owen and me and smiled. "I don't think your grandmother has ever been late."

"Our gram isn't coming today. Our mother is . . . was coming," I said. My voice seemed to be shrinking.

"Your mother? But I thought . . ." said Ms. Domínguez. She gave Ms. Morimoto one of those raised-eyebrow looks.

"Mrs. Outlaw called this morning," said Ms. Morimoto. "She told me the children's mother was in town and was coming to the conference and bringing them home afterward."

"Our mother came back for a visit," said Owen, but the usual luster was gone from his voice and his face. He looked pitiful standing there in his rumpled vest and tie.

"Ah . . ." said Ms. Domínguez. "Well, it's pretty late and it's getting dark. . . ."

"You can call Fabiola and Bernardo," I said, remembering that Gram was working on those bridesmaid dresses.

"The neighbors," Ms. Morimoto explained to Ms. Domínguez. "They're the emergency contacts. I would make the call myself, but . . ." Ms. Morimoto looked down at my hand, clutching tight to hers.

Ms. Domínguez nodded. She called and we went back to the steps to wait.

Ten minutes later Gram pulled up in the Toyota.

I let go of Ms. Morimoto's hand and started toward the car. As soon as I reached the curb, I realized I had left my backpack in the hall, near the school office.

I hurried back to get it and as I hoisted it onto my back, I heard Ms. Morimoto's voice from inside: ". . . called yesterday to give me some history on the mother. She's been in and out of rehab hospitals and halfway houses for years. Severe alcohol abuse and the irrational behaviors that go along with it."

"Is she on medication?" asked Ms. Domínguez.

"Apparently she hasn't been drinking lately and is taking

meds for her moods," said Ms. Morimoto. "But you know the story. Once they start up again, it's a vicious circle. I just hate to think of that woman getting close to Naomi and Owen. Those children were standing in the wrong line when they passed out mothers."

"Whatever happened to the father?"

"There's no contact. He and the mother are divorced. Mrs. Outlaw said he wanted the children at one time, but the mother wouldn't allow it. He lives in Mexico."

I hurried away. Rehab hospitals and halfway houses. What *was* a halfway house, anyway? Medicine for moods. Was Skyla sick? And my father . . . he wanted us?

At first, hearing about him was like a pinch, reminding me of someone else who hadn't come to get me. But the part about him wanting us, that was like a found piece of candy when you didn't even know you were craving something sweet.

Why hadn't Gram told us?

8 a burden of mules

"Lemon Tree is already decorating for Christmas, and Thanksgiving is still a week away. They start earlier every year," said Gram when we got into the car. She was talking in that I'm-just-making-conversation voice.

I stared straight ahead with my arms crossed and didn't say a word. Neither did Owen. When Gram turned right instead of left at the corner, I knew we were headed for Spray 'n Play, Gram's destination after any difficulty or cause for celebration. Outside, the play area had one of those padded climbing gyms, and inside, the deli had a soft-serve ice-cream counter with all the toppings. Our favorite thing to do was to fix sundaes and sit in front of the giant picture window, which looked directly into the car wash, the part where the cars rolled through on the track.

It was fine to go there after Owen had a particularly bad day at physical therapy, or to celebrate if I got a good grade on a test. But did Gram really think that ice cream would make up for Skyla leaving us again?

I pressed my nose to the car window. A vacant lot had been fenced with chain link and a big sign read, "Trees Coming Soon." A few store windows had already been frosted like cakes with spray-on snow. Colored Christmas lights sparkled on the eaves of some of the buildings. In front of a church, a man struggled to lift a life-size plastic Mary with child onto a plastic donkey for a giant Nativity scene. The donkey looked much too small for its load.

I saw a family walking down the street. The mom pushed a stroller with a young girl snuggled inside, happily holding a stuffed doll. The father wore a baby backpack with a little boy perched on his shoulders. The mother laughed, and the father leaned over and kissed her. If Skyla hadn't been having problems with alcohol and if our father had come back to Lemon Tree, would that have been us?

Gram parked the Toyota at Spray 'n Play. My arms still crossed and head hunched over, I followed her and Owen inside. The clerk stood in front of the soft-serve machine with pieces of the insides unassembled on the counter in front of her. "Sorry," she said, shrugging her shoulders when she saw us. "I'm cleaning the dispensers."

We walked over toward the car wash area. A big sign had been taped to the viewing window. "Closed for Repairs." Two men in overalls worked on the other side of the window, tinkering with the spray nozzles. We sat down at a table near the picture window anyway.

Gram sent Owen to buy three ready-made ice-cream sandwiches. "I guess it's just not our lucky day," she said.

I ignored her. It seemed Owen's found penny had been wrong.

When Owen came back with the ice cream, I let mine sit on the table and melt. Owen and Gram ate theirs in silence, and then the three of us peered through the car wash window into the quiet of the stock-still machinery.

"It's not going to start up no matter how hard we stare. A watched pot doesn't boil, although, Naomi, I've been sitting here watching you and you look like you're going to burst."

Our entire life Gram had been tight-lipped about anything to do with our parents. If Owen asked, "What was our mother like?" Gram always answered, "That's best left unsaid. Let's focus on the future." If I asked about our father, Gram said, "Naomi, let's not dredge up the river bottom." Didn't she know that Owen and I had a million questions?

Finally I turned to face her. "We waited and waited. Owen wore a suit and tie! Blanca and her mother waited, too! What's rehab and a halfway house? Is Skyla sick? And what about our father? I thought he didn't want us but he did!"

Deliberately and at a snail's pace, Gram wiped her hands with a napkin. She always went into slow motion when she was putting her thoughts in order. "A rehab hospital is a place people go to recover from alcoholism, from letting alcohol mess up their lives. I'm sorry to say that Skyla has been in several. When she gets out of a rehab hospital, she has to go into a halfway house for a while. It's a house where people learn how to live in the real world again, but with counselors watching over them. And sometimes, after a lot of years, drinking makes a person's brain work cattywampus and doctors have to give them medicine to straighten it out, so they can handle their everyday problems."

"Why didn't you tell us?" I asked.

"I didn't know until she showed up here last week. She asked me not to mention it to you," said Gram. "I was giving Skyla the benefit of making a clean start with her life . . . and with you kids. She admitted she'd made a lot of bad decisions and pointed out that the one good decision she had made was to leave you children with me, and well . . . I guess I hung my hat on the prospect that she had pulled herself together."

"What about our father?" I said. "Ms. Morimoto told Ms. Domínguez that our father wanted us, but Skyla wouldn't let him see us."

Gram took a deep breath. "So much happened back then. . . . I've carried it too long. The night of the storm, after Santiago saved you from the flooded motel, he went to move his boat to the harbor but got caught in the hurricane. His motor broke and the boat was blown south into a cove, where he was stranded for over a week. When he finally got help and a tow back to Rosarito, he went straight back to the church, but Skyla had already left with you two."

I watched the melted ice cream drip from the table to the floor.

"Santiago called my house right away. He and Skyla had some heated phone calls, all fights and fury. After one of the calls, she tore every picture of your father to shreds. She told him in no uncertain terms that if he tried to contact you, she'd take him to court. It was all bluster, but Santiago didn't know that. I'm sure the poor man was fed up with her shenanigans. After that I didn't hear from him for several years. Then one day he started sending money orders in care of me, for you both. He sends a sizable amount a couple of times a year."

A surge of frustration welled up inside of me. Why did grown-ups always think that kids couldn't understand the truth? With Skyla showing up and all this new information about my father, I might as well have been lugging around a giant suitcase filled with rocks for the weariness that settled on my shoulders.

"We could have written him a letter to tell him we were with you," I said.

"I tried that, Naomi. I wrote a half-dozen letters, but they all came back to me. And none of his money order envelopes ever had a return address."

"You could have at least told us." I buried my head in Gram's lap and started to cry.

Gram patted my back. "He was a fisherman and sometimes spent weeks out on his boat. That was no life for you kids. By the time I got Owen set up with his doctors and you with the counselor, I was so attached that I didn't want to take the tiniest chance of losing either one of you. After my letters came back, I didn't try anymore. That was selfish on my part. You can blame me for that."

Just then a big noise echoed from inside the car wash, interrupting my cry. I sat up. The machinery churned on the other side of the viewing window and a car headed through on the track. Tiny jets sprayed foamy soaps and waxes in rainbow colors on the car. Then the giant machinery went to work scrubbing and lathering. Finally, fingerlike water nozzles waved back and forth, rinsing off the suds.

Owen tapped me on the shoulder. "You can stop now, Naomi. They got the car wash working."

He and Gram laughed, but I couldn't summon a smile. We watched a few cars go through the wash.

"Any more nettles in your cap?" asked Gram, taking my hand.

I looked up at her. "What's a vicious circle?"

Skyla never came home the night of the conference. Three nights later, Gram, Owen, and I had cleaned the kitchen from Sunday pot roast and arranged ourselves comfy on the sofa to watch television.

That's when Skyla's car pulled up and her horn beeped. Gram tensed, and Owen and I sat still as statues.

A few minutes later, the door popped open. "Come outside, everyone," Skyla said all cheerful. "I have a surprise and news. Which do you want first?"

Was she really going to act like nothing happened?

Gram demanded, "Have you lost your mind? Why didn't you go to the conferences and pick these children up from school on Thursday?"

Skyla didn't blink. She just stared at Gram and said, "Something came up. Sorry. Don't you want to hear my news?"

"These children were counting on you to show up," continued Gram. "Their teachers had appointments with you. Naomi and Owen waited on the steps of the school until dark! Where *were* you?"

Skyla tilted her head and look confused. "Clive and I went to Palm Springs for a long weekend. That's all. Now, my news is that I invited Clive to come for Thanksgiving and he said yes. He is dying to meet you all. Isn't that great?"

Skyla looked from me to Owen to Gram. I was sure

we looked like a jury sitting all in a row on the sofa. "What? Are you all going to ruin everything by holding it against me that I skipped two little conferences? I can't believe it! Obviously everyone got home just fine and no harm was done. That is just like you, Gram. You were always this way, raining on all of my joy. And it looks like you've taught these children your same pitiful attitude. Well, I am not going to let you spoil my spirit. Now, out in my car is a big present and I have been counting the minutes to get it here, but I can just as easily return it, if that's what you want!"

She turned and walked out, slamming the door.

Gram closed her eyes and shook her head, talking to the ceiling. "How does she always turn things around in her favor?"

"Can we go look?" asked Owen. "Please?"

Gram finally nodded, and Owen and I bolted outside.

Skyla opened the trunk of the car and struggled to pull something out. A few seconds later she wheeled a brand-new bicycle into the halo of porch light.

I sucked in my breath.

The tags and a helmet dangled from the handlebars and the blue metallic paint shimmered. It had all the expensive extras: a light, fancy reflectors, and a leather pack behind the seat.

"A bike!" said Owen, clapping the sides of his cheeks and jumping up and down.

"Isn't it beautiful?" said Skyla. "Owen, it's a present for you, from Clive. He wants to meet all of you, and this is his way of introducing himself. Well?"

Gram was flat-out staring at Skyla in disbelief, with her mouth so wide open that she was going to catch flies if she didn't shut it soon.

Skyla beamed.

"Thank you, thank you, thank you!" Owen said it so loud, I was sure everyone at Avocado Acres heard him. He was already balanced on the seat, with Gram holding the handlebars. He couldn't ride it yet because it needed to be adjusted for his height, and he needed a little block of wood on one of the pedals so his legs would be even. Gram wheeled him away down toward the blacktop as he called, "Thank youuuuuu!"

I was so happy for Owen that I wanted to hug Skyla. But she leaned against the car, looking after him, and she wasn't smiling. Her arms were crossed tight, not inviting affection.

"Thank you for buying Owen the bike," I said, my voice a whisper.

Skyla glared at me. "Naomi, why can't you speak up? When Clive comes over for Thanksgiving, I expect you to tell *him* loud and clear 'Thank you very much' for all his thoughtfulness." She continued with a short, clipped voice. "He paid for that bike and everything else. He wants to be friends with you, especially, and I'm counting on you doing the same in return for all he's done. You owe him that, so don't disappoint me. Do you understand me, young lady?"

I quickly nodded and backed away from Skyla, then turned and ran after Gram and Owen. Was I in trouble? Why did Clive want to be my friend? Why did I have to tell him thank you loud and clear? I didn't want to owe him anything.

I caught up to Owen and Gram and took over pushing the bike. As I wheeled Owen around the trailer park loop, a troublesome feeling tiptoed after me like a lurking shadow.

"I guess that's the best we can do to dress up this dump," said Skyla, standing in the living room/kitchen on Thanksgiving morning. She surveyed Owen's construction paper turkeys and cornucopias taped in the window. "I am leaving for Clive's now, but we'll be back at two o'clock for dinner. Now remember what I told you about thanking him, Naomi."

I half smiled and nodded to her as she headed out the door. I etched a few more feathers on the bird I had carved. Gram had a gnarled manzanita branch she decorated for the different holidays, and she thought that if I trimmed it with some of my carvings it would show them off and make a fitting and conversational Thanksgiving centerpiece. I chose the best of my herd of animals, nestling some of the figures among the twisted curlicues and hanging others from thread on the mangled twigs.

"Naomi, what has gotten into you?" said Gram. "I am

worried you're going to faint from that irregular breathing! You're not fretting on that figure, are you?"

I wasn't worried about the new carving, but the prospect of meeting Clive had me trying to fill my lungs with confidence. Between breaths, I held up the soap and admired it. It was the first time I'd ever carved a bird with the wings in the flying position, and even I could see it was the prettiest and most delicate thing I'd ever done. I set it on the uppermost twig of the manzanita, like an angel on a Christmas tree.

"That looks dandy," said Gram. "The new carving reminds me of a bluebird of happiness, the way the wings are out and all. Now, let's get out my yellow-checked tablecloth. I hope it doesn't clash with Mrs. Maloney. Then I'll baste that turkey."

I headed for the cupboard to get the tablecloth. Maybe if I looked hard enough I could find all eight cloth napkins that matched. I wanted us all to sit down and have dinner like those families in Gram's lady magazines. The ones in the photos, passing the food with smiles on their faces and oozing politeness. I didn't want to disappoint Skyla, though lately it was hard making things right for her, let alone the mysterious Clive. I took another deep breath. What if I couldn't say thank you? What if he didn't like me?

Clive was big, like a mountain. Not fat, exactly, but broad and thick. I looked for tattoos, but he was wearing a leather jacket. Pulled back into a ponytail, his black hair looked dyed and it was wrinkled into waves of tight lines. The first thing that popped into my mind was that his hair had been French braided and slept in overnight, then let out.

He shook hands with Owen and me and gave Gram a poinsettia that dangled a $3.98 grocery store tag. Then he redirected his attention to Skyla, keeping his arm around her waist. He reached up and patted her hair, which wasn't raven brown anymore. A few nights ago she had bought a box of Pumpkin Spice hair color at the pharmacy and did a makeover. She had also found a lipstick called Pumpkin Pie that was a dead-on match.

Mrs. Maloney arrived, toting her lime gelatin salad with little marshmallows. She wore her pink-checked robe, but in honor of the occasion she had added a rhinestone turkey pin near the top button. Fabiola and Bernardo came with pots of stuffing, mashed potatoes, and Fabiola's specialty, cranberry sauce with jalapeño peppers.

Lulu took one look at Clive and started barking. We all knew she'd settle down, but Clive backed away from her and the more he backed away, the more Lulu inched forward.

"Get that dog away from me. I don't like dogs. Skyla, you *know* how I feel about dogs."

"Clive has issues with dogs," explained Skyla.

Gram walked over, picked up Lulu, and said, "Why, this dog wouldn't bite a biscuit!"

Bernardo took Lulu from Gram and walked her back to their house. We could hear Lulu's whining all the way through the grove.

After Bernardo came back and the food was situated, we all sat down at the patio table and Mrs. Maloney's borrowed card table, which we'd pushed together and covered with Gram's tablecloth.

Mrs. Maloney said grace and ended with, ". . . and I am thankful for my neighbors, who always take such good care of me, and for this beautiful weather, which allows us to sit outside on Thanksgiving Day while others are freezing in some parts of the country. Amen."

"Please eat while the food is hot," said Gram, passing the candied yams.

As the food circled the table, Clive picked up the bluebird from the manzanita branch and said, "This soap?"

"Naomi carved it herself," said Gram. "It's a hobby of hers. We think she has a natural gift."

"Their father was *obsessed* with carving," said Skyla, patting Clive on the arm. "And not in a good way. Every year he left me for a week right before Christmas to go to some carving thing in Mexico. Imagine leaving a wife and kids at that time of year!"

"*La Noche de los Rábanos,*" said Bernardo proudly. "In Oaxaca."

"Yeah, the radish night," said Owen. Bernardo had told us about the festival many times.

"I don't think I've ever heard of anything like that," said Mrs. Maloney.

Bernardo continued. "Those who work with wood come to Oaxaca City from all over the state to carve beautiful scenes out of radishes."

"They use not only the little salad radishes," said Fabiola, "but also giant radishes, the size of arms and legs, a special type the government grows for the festival."

"For over a hundred years, families have entered the competition," said Bernardo. "León, it is a famous carving family in Oaxaca. Naomi has the heart of a carver, like her father."

Clive sort of grunted and set the bird down on the table, next to his napkin.

"All I remember is that those painted wooden animals were everywhere," said Skyla. "He wouldn't even let me buy a store-bought mobile for above Owen's crib. Instead, he took an old branch and nailed it to the ceiling and hung those things from it. I'd forgotten about all that nonsense until now. Do we have to talk about this? Mrs. Maloney, have you always lived here?"

As I spooned stuffing onto my plate, I remembered that colorful swirl above my head in the motel room in Mexico. It hadn't been a dream after all. I tucked it away in my mind to think about later.

"Yes, I've always lived in Lemon Tree," said Mrs. Maloney. She turned to Clive. "And where are your people from?"

He stopped chewing on a turkey leg. "I don't have contact with anyone, and that's by choice, except a daughter from my second marriage. She's a couple years younger than Naomi."

Everyone nodded, real polite.

Fabiola asked, "What is her name?"

"Her name was Elizabeth, but I renamed her Sapphire. Could someone pass the mashed potatoes?"

"Isn't Sapphire a beautiful name?" said Skyla.

"In all my life I never heard of such a thing," said Mrs. Maloney. "Elizabeth is a perfectly fine name."

Gram always said that when you're eighty-eight years old, you can say whatever you like.

Clive concentrated on pouring gravy over his pile of potatoes. "Her mother named her Elizabeth after her own mother, who I didn't like. I thought she should be called something I could enjoy, especially since she's coming to live with me when I move to Las Vegas after my training."

"Isn't that great?" said Skyla.

"What about Sapphire's mother?" asked Gram.

"She'll still get to see Sapphire on vacations and some weekends," said Clive. "I proved that living with me was better for Sapphire. Besides, her mother wasn't responsible with the state money, always spending too much on the kid."

"State money?" said Gram.

"The state supplement for dependents," said Clive, rubbing his hands together like a fly on a sandwich. "If you have custody of a minor and you don't make much money, the government helps you out with a little extra every month. Free Legal Aid told me everything I needed to know to qualify."

"Naomi, Clive and I decided that you are the perfect friend for Sapphire, being a little older and all," said Skyla. "You could watch out for her like a big sister. You're going to meet her real soon. Won't that be fun? Take a trip to Las Vegas?" Skyla was looking around the table with bright eyes and a smile, like she'd just had the most sincerely tremendous idea.

Suddenly I couldn't swallow.

Fabiola and Bernardo looked at Skyla with curiosity. Gram stared at her and narrowed her eyes, nodding her head ever so slightly.

The only one eating was Clive.

Mrs. Maloney set down her fork. "We couldn't do without Naomi here, not for a minute."

"Anyway," said Owen, "she's got school."

"They've got plenty of schools in Las Vegas," said Clive. "So that's not a problem." He took off his leather jacket and tossed it on the patio couch. A tattoo of a shark, teeth bared and dripping blood, bulged on his forearm muscle.

An uncomfortable silence like a thick fog sneaked its way around the turkey platter, circled the mashed potatoes, and rose up in a cloud above the lime gelatin salad. It was the kind of quiet when you hoped somebody would say any little thing.

My fork started to chatter against my plate.

Gram reached over to steady my hand. "Naomi, help me carry these dishes inside so we can make room for dessert. I made pecan and pumpkin pies."

I picked up my plate and followed Gram. Unfortunately Clive was right behind us, clutching his napkin.

"Which way to the bathroom? I need to wash up."

Gram pointed down the hall. When he was out of sight, she whispered, "Don't you pay any mind to that nonsense out there. Now, go get me a few more plates."

Gram kept me busy with the dishes, but I couldn't stop thinking about Skyla wanting to take me to Las Vegas. I wasn't going anywhere without Owen and Gram. My idea was that Skyla would move somewhere close by us — maybe to a cute, little apartment — and Owen and I could visit her, stopping in from school on our way home. Home to Baby Beluga and Gram.

When I came back in with the last of the plates, Clive was sitting in the living room/kitchen, leaning back on the bench seat with his hands folded behind his head.

Gram rinsed the plates and stacked them on top of each other with a loud clink.

"This trailer isn't half bad," he said.

"It's not much, but it's what I can afford and it's the children's home," said Gram, her voice tight.

"But you must get money from the state," said Clive. "That's got to be a bundle for two kids, right? And what's the story on the little old lady outside? Is she your dependent, too?" He was kind of half smirking at Gram.

I stopped scraping the plates. Gram did not take to people prying into her personals.

Gram slammed a plate down so hard it broke, the pieces clattering into the sink. She turned to face Clive and straightened up as tall as she could muster. Unfortunately she was not wearing her athletic shoes, and even sitting down, Clive seemed to tower over her. "I think you're asking an awful lot of someone you just met, and I don't think it's any of your business. And Mrs. Maloney is a friend, plain and simple."

Just then Skyla walked in. "Have you all been making nice?" she asked.

Gram never took her eyes from Clive's face. "Clive was just inquiring into my finances, seeing how we're such good friends and all. He wants to know how much money I get each month for Naomi and Owen and I'd like to know why he's so interested in something I've never asked for." Gram shook her head. "What you see is what we've got. And for your information, Naomi is not going to Las Vegas to be a baby-sitter or otherwise. I won't have it."

Clive stared at the floor. He seemed mad.

Skyla looked at him and raised her eyebrows and pursed her mouth. She grabbed his hand. "Clive, this isn't the time or the place. Come on outside and sit down and have dessert."

Gram stared after them. "Naomi, would you run and fetch my sweater from my bed? There's a chill outside."

As I passed the bathroom, I noticed something wadded up on the edge of the sink. It was Clive's napkin. Next to it a brown-streaked lump of soap sat in a puddle of water. He had taken my bluebird of happiness from the Thanksgiving table and used it to wash the turkey grease from his hands.

After the contentment of the pies had set in, Owen and Bernardo laid out the checkerboard.

"Who wants to play?" asked Owen.

I glanced at Bernardo and smiled. Owen could beat most adults.

"I'll play," said Skyla.

They played three games in a row and Skyla won each

time. After every game she whooped and hollered and yelled, "I won!"

Owen just sat there, grinning a happy face. "Want to play again?"

I had never once seen Owen lose to anyone. I looked at Bernardo, and he shrugged his shoulders.

Gram said, "Skyla, why would any grown-up take that much delight in winning over a small child?"

"He needs to learn how to compete. He needs to learn how to use his brain. Set 'em up again, Owen, and let's see you try harder."

"He couldn't get any smarter," said Gram.

"Oh, I know," said Skyla, patting Owen on the head like he was a dog.

I could tell that Skyla didn't believe Gram. "He gets straight 'A's," I said.

"Naomi, that's real sweet of you to stick up for your brother. I'm the same way with people, always trying to make them feel better. That's why you and me are two peas in a pod."

"Did it ever occur to you, Skyla," said Gram, "that he could beat you at any time and maybe he's just trying to please you?"

Skyla smiled. "I won fair and square. Right, Owen?"

Owen looked at all of us, who knew better. "Sort of," he said.

The sweetness left Skyla's face and her eyes narrowed. "You mean you've been letting me win?"

Owen's gigantic smile slipped into a guilty, sad-eyed face.

"I don't like people making fun of me, Owen, so play like you mean it." Skyla quickly set up the board, and it took Owen a matter of minutes to win.

She sat back and glared at Owen. "Just think how smart people would think you were, if you didn't have that tape plastered all over your chest and if you wore a lift in your shoe so you'd walk even, like everybody else. Wouldn't that give a better impression?"

Owen said, "I had a lift in my shoe once, but the doctors have to make me a taller one because I'm growing.

It's coming next month . . . and then . . . and then I'll be even . . . right, Gram?" His voice trailed off.

Before Gram could answer, Clive said, "Hey, let me play, buddy. I love checkers." He signaled for Skyla to go sit on the couch.

For a minute I was grateful to him for getting Owen away from Skyla.

Owen set up the board and beat Clive three games running.

Clive looked up at Skyla. "This kid's an ace. I'd put a ton of money on him and have him play some dudes I know. We could make a fortune."

"You'd bet on Owen?" said Gram.

"Just for fun," said Clive, shrugging his shoulders.

"I get it," said Skyla. "To look at him, you wouldn't think he had a brain in his body or could beat anybody at anything, especially with him being crippled —"

"Skyla!" said Gram.

Bernardo stood up and walked over to Owen. He quietly put the checkers and board back in the box and took

Owen's hand, leading him toward his house through the avocado trees.

Mrs. Maloney turned to Skyla and said, "Shame on you!"

"All I'm saying," said Skyla, "is that he doesn't *look* smart and that could work in Clive's favor. You know what I mean. Owen's not right physically, and he has weird habits."

"And you needed to point that out to him on Thanksgiving Day in front of all these people?" said Gram. "He still has doctor appointments every three months to see what can be done for him. Another one a week from today. Maybe you should consider coming along to see what this child is up against." Gram looked at Skyla and shook her head in disgust. "Mrs. Maloney, let me walk you home. It's almost five o'clock, and I know you'll be wanting to go to bed soon."

Fabiola started folding up Mrs. Maloney's chairs.

Gram told me, "Naomi, run over and get Lulu. I cooked

the turkey giblets for her, and it wouldn't be Thanksgiving if she didn't get to eat them. Clive, there's no need to leave on Lulu's account. She's *usually* a fair judge of folks."

Clive grabbed Skyla's hand and they headed toward the car.

Before I reached the grove, Skyla called out, "Naomi! Aren't you forgetting something?"

I felt my breath catch in my throat. I turned back and walked toward the Mustang, practicing the line I'd rehearsed. Skyla and Clive were already situated in the car, seatbelts buckled, and watching my every move. My throat tightened like it always did when people stared at me.

I leaned down and peeked in the passenger window and choked out the words. "Thank . . . you . . . for . . . all the nice . . . things you bought us."

Clive didn't answer. His chin raised up and down once. I guessed that meant, "You're welcome."

I stood up and, glancing in the back, saw a twelve-pack of beer on the seat. Was Skyla drinking again? If she was, what would that mean? That she'd have to go back to a halfway house? Or to the hospital?

Skyla's eyes turned hard and squinty. "That's my business, Naomi, not yours. If you know what's good for you, you'll keep your mouth shut."

"That's weird. Absolutely weird," said Blanca after I told her about Thanksgiving Day on the way to class Monday morning. "Clive sounds scary. Don't you feel sorry for his daughter?"

I nodded. "I'm not going to Las Vegas. Gram said it loud and clear."

"Did you tell her about the booze in the backseat?"

"No . . . well . . . I didn't know for sure if Skyla was really going to drink it. I mean . . . maybe it was just for Clive. Gram has enough worries right now. And then what if Gram says something to Skyla and Skyla gets mad at me?"

"Skyla wouldn't have told you to keep your mouth shut if the beer was for Clive. You should tell your gram," said Blanca.

"No," I said. "Not until I know for sure." I could already hear the caterwaul of Skyla and Gram fighting if Gram found out.

"Naomi the Lion," said Blanca, shaking her head as we

walked into Ms. Morimoto's room. "You need to wake up before something bad happens."

"We have a problem," said Gram, rushing into the trailer on Thursday afternoon. "I'm going to have to cancel Owen's appointment."

"Why?" said Skyla, brushing her baby finger with Holly Berry nail polish.

"The bride of that big wedding is at Fabiola's," said Gram. "She tried on the wedding gown and has lost so much weight that we're going to have to work straight through the afternoon to get it altered. The wedding is this weekend, out of town. She's coming back first thing in the morning to pick up the gown."

"I can take Owen," said Skyla, waving her hands to dry her nails.

Gram's forehead wrinkled.

"Now, don't look so worried or be like you used to be, not trusting me over every little thing. I'll even pick up

Chicken in a Bucket for dinner. We can handle it, can't we, Naomi?"

For the past week Skyla had been smooth and nice as cream pie. She hadn't once mentioned Las Vegas again. Maybe if she helped Gram today, it would mend just about everything between them.

"I'll take notes for you just like always," I said to Gram, holding up my notebook. "And I'll call you *the minute* we get home."

Gram hesitated and bit her lip. "Well . . . it would be a big help. Otherwise we'd have to wait forever for another appointment. And it's just his usual X ray and consultation."

"For heaven's sake," said Skyla. "It's only to Children's Hospital and back. Now, it's all decided. Besides, I *am* his mother."

Owen and I knew Children's Hospital by heart and could give directions to anyone for surgery, pediatrics, physical therapy, orthopedics, and the lab. I had sat in just about every waiting room and visited all the public restrooms. We'd spent so much time here over the years that Gram said they should name a table in the cafeteria after us.

At every nurses' station we passed, someone said hello to us or came out to slap hands with Owen, or to give me a hug and to ask about Gram. While Owen was in radiology getting his X rays, Skyla and I waited in the hall in plastic chairs. Wide eyed, she watched each doctor and nurse walk by.

When an orderly pushed a patient down the hall in a bed on wheels, Skyla shuddered. "Hospitals give me the creeps."

"Why?" I asked. "Lots of people get better in hospitals."

"Yeah, well, lots of people don't," she snapped. She got up and paced. "Naomi, *when* are you going to start talking so I can hear you? I am tired of straining my ears. Hand me my purse and tell me in a regular voice where I can find the restroom."

Raising my voice a hair, I said, "It's down the hall to the right."

She jerked her purse out of my hand and marched off. When she finally came back twenty minutes later, she had double-dosed herself with gardenia perfume. Layered underneath was something even stronger. It reminded me of Gram's Christmas rum cake.

I coughed and choked on all the sweetness. "What's that smell?"

"Naomi, it's just a little something to calm me down. To get me through all this." She looked around the hospital hallway. "You mind your own business, like I told you before. Do you hear me?"

I nodded, looking at my shoes. She *was* drinking again. But no matter what she said, the alcohol wasn't relaxing her because her hands shook and she could not stand still.

After the X rays, the three of us waited in one of the fancy consult rooms with nice furniture. Gram called them friendly rooms. She said that if the doctors gave you bad news, they wanted you in a comfy, friendly atmosphere, not a scary one. Skyla sat down and tapped her nails on the table. The room had a window looking into a small playroom

where the doctors would ask Owen to go when they were
ready to report the grown-up stuff. They always let me
stay, since I was Gram's secretary.

"How much longer?" said Skyla.

"A few minutes," said Owen.

"Good, then I have time to scoot out to the restroom."

When she came back, the perfume was taking a backseat
to the rum cake.

Two doctors arrived wearing white smocks and holding
file folders. Little koala bears hugged their stethoscopes,
and one wore a tie with bright balloons all over it. Owen
jumped up and hugged them. They were part of his special
team.

After they let go of Owen, Dr. Reed turned to us.
"Hello, Naomi. And you must be Owen's mother" — she
looked at his folder — "Skyla Jones. Mrs. Outlaw called
and said you'd be bringing him today. I'm Dr. Amanda
Reed, and this is my colleague, Dr. John Navarro. I'm an
orthopedist and Dr. Navarro is an ENT. We both specialize
in pediatrics."

Owen leaned toward Skyla and whispered. "She's a bone doctor and he's an ear, nose, and throat guy, and they take care of kids."

Skyla glared at him. "I *know* what they are, Owen." Her voice sounded pinched. She tapped a little harder on the table, and one of her press-on nails flew across the room and landed on the floor.

Owen laughed hard and the doctors chuckled along with him. When Owen saw Skyla's stare, he immediately stopped.

I tried to cover my smile with my hands.

Skyla's face was as hot as her nail polish. "What can you do about Owen?" she said, examining her fingers.

Skyla didn't know the order of things.

"First, we'd like Owen to be excused. Why don't you go to the playroom for a few minutes while we talk," said Dr. Reed.

After Owen hopped up and went into the adjoining room, Dr. Navarro turned to Skyla. "At this juncture, there is nothing more to do. He's had all the surgeries that his age and size can accommodate. There's a surgery we would like to do when he reaches adolescence, when he's thirteen or fourteen, but for now, we've reviewed all of his tests and we've determined that he's in great shape. He's just going to be an FLK."

"A what?" said Skyla.

"A Funny Looking Kid," said Dr. Reed.

"Is that some medical term, or are you trying to make a joke?"

"No," said Dr. Navarro. "I'm most certainly not making fun of him. And sometimes it's a term we use unofficially. He's fine mentally. In fact, he has a rather high IQ and is quite bright. He just has a few physical problems that were the result of his birth defects, but there's nothing more we can do surgically, *for now.* He's just going to be —"

"An FLK. A Funny Looking Kid?" said Skyla, her voice rising, scary and shrill. "As if I don't have enough problems! This is . . . is . . . embarrassing!"

Dr. Reed wrinkled her forehead. "He's healthy and has

a wonderful outlook on life. He has great prospects, great potential, and with a few more surgeries when he gets older . . ."

I didn't think Owen would mind being a Funny Looking Kid for a few more years. We had both spent enough time at Children's Hospital to know that his ailments were slight compared to some others. If Gram were here, she would have said it was our lucky day.

Skyla pressed her lips together tight. She leaned toward the doctors and said, "This kid's a Blem. He's crooked and he can't talk right, and you're telling me nothing more can be done to make him right. Well, that's no bargain in my book!"

I couldn't believe that Skyla was comparing Owen to Walker Gordon's once yearly sale of discount shoes called Blems, the ones with flaws.

Dr. Navarro searched in his pocket, pulled out a business card, stood up, and handed it to Skyla. "Ms. Jones, please call me if you have any questions. I'd be happy to talk to you at length, and I can also recommend a support group if you like. We know Owen rather well and he's a remarkable young man. My number is on the card."

Skyla looked at the card and tossed it back on the table. Then she stood up, walked over to the playroom door, and jerked it open. "Owen, come on! We're getting out of here!"

Owen walked into the conference room, smiling, until he saw all the concerned looks around him. I got up and took his hand. "Everything's okay, Owen."

"Naomi!" yelled Skyla. "Everything is *not* okay!"

As we left the room, I saw Owen eyeing the tape dispenser on the shelf near the door.

Skyla kept her eyes straight on the road and barely moved all the way home, except for her swigs from one of those plastic travel bottles that she kept pulling out of her purse. Even though it was dark, she drove too fast, weaving the car in and out of traffic. Owen pulled himself so far into his hooded sweatshirt, he looked like a swaddled cocoon. When we finally arrived at Baby Beluga, I was dizzy and my hands trembled. As soon as I got inside, I hurried to call Gram.

Skyla said, "Put the phone down, Naomi. Sit down, both of you."

We sat.

"Don't you *ever* laugh at me or humiliate me like that again! And Naomi, don't give me that 'I don't know what you're talking about' stare, because you know exactly what I mean. Owen, I guess there's not much to be done with you, but you're going to stop this tape thing starting right now. And if you don't, that bike is going in the trash."

"Gram always lets me have tape," said Owen, his voice hoarse. "I can wear it if I want."

Let it be, Owen. Please let it be, I prayed.

"I'm your mother, Owen, and if I say it's going to stop, it's going to stop." Skyla took a step toward Owen.

I was a shaking leaf but my instincts moved my body right between Owen and Skyla. I said, "It doesn't *hurt* anything."

Skyla stared at me with fire and hammers. The phone rang and she answered it, never taking her eyes from mine.

"Hi, baby," said Skyla. "Saturday, that's great! I'll start packing up right now and I'll be over later. I'm not staying in this hole one more minute. . . . Don't worry, she'll come along, just like we planned. No . . . I don't care what you say, I am not bringing him, not after the day I've had. . . . I never could handle that situation and I still can't. Tell you about it later."

Skyla hung up and headed straight for the cupboard under the kitchen sink and pulled out a plastic garbage bag. She walked around the living room/kitchen, picking up her things and tossing them inside the bag. Then she headed to the bedroom. From the back of the trailer, she yelled, "I can't find Rose Tulip! Where's my Rose Tulip lipstick? Naomi, you haven't been using it, have you?"

Skyla hurried down the hall toward us, dragging the bag.

"Clive's job came through in Las Vegas, finally. We're

leaving, Naomi. Toss some things in this bag. Bring those jeans I bought you and those sparkly shirts."

Leaving? I wasn't leaving. I shook my head.

"Don't tell me no! I have had it with your attitude and your only saying two words and speaking-in-whispers nonsense. Where did I put that lipstick?" Skyla began poking around the shelf above the sink. When she turned and saw I wasn't moving, she yelled, "Get your things right now!" and swept her hand across the shelf. The three little soap ducks fell to the floor, their heads breaking off and rolling around like tops. I looked down at the broken pieces.

"You . . . you can't tell us what to do," I said. Where were my words coming from?

Skyla bristled. "I can tell you to do anything I like. I'm your mother. I can see that Gram obviously doesn't know how to raise children. Just look at you, with your smart mouth."

A mean, stomp-my-foot feeling rose from a place I didn't know existed in my mind. I wished I could throw my anger at Skyla and yell, but my voice came out a shaky whimper. "Gram takes care of us. She does . . . *everything* for us. Not like you. You *left* us. You didn't . . . *want* . . . us and then you didn't even let our father see us. Now we're supposed to do what you s-s-say? I . . . I . . . I'm . . . n-n-*not* . . . going."

Skyla took two steps across the room, then slapped me across the cheek.

It was such a hard slap that my head turned and snapped against my shoulder. I didn't have to look in a mirror to know that the sting of her hand was perfectly imprinted. I felt it from the inside out.

Angry, burning tears stung my eyes. I wanted to wipe them away, but now my hands were paralyzed and my feet were rooted to the floor.

Skyla raised her hand again.

"Leave her alone!" yelled Owen, running over and throwing his arms around my waist.

Skyla dropped her hand. Spooky calm words came from her mouth. "There's more where that came from,

Naomi. I can see that I'm going to need to spend a lot of time teaching you how to mind. And don't give me those puppy-dog eyes like you're scared of me. I always hated it when you did that. I can't believe you haven't changed one bit since you were little, always defying me then and still defying me now. You know, if anything happens to Gram, all you'll have is me anyway, and something could happen to her any time now, old as she is. You wouldn't want that, would you, Naomi? Something bad happening to Gram on account of you?"

My knees went gelatin wobbly. What was Skyla saying? That she would hurt Gram? That she might kill Gram? I was still trying to grasp it all when her voice switched to sugar.

"Now, Naomi honey, you know I didn't mean that little slap, so don't hold it against me. You are just like me, remember? Two peas in a pod. It will be fun. You can go to school in Las Vegas. Clive has Sapphire now, so you'll have a friend that's like a little sister. It's been all arranged and decided. We're picking her up on the way. Owen's going to stay here and take care of Gram, so you see, everyone will be happy."

I started inching toward the door.

Skyla swooped like a hawk diving for a morsel of meat and grabbed my arm, digging her nails into my skin.

I flinched. Skyla was wrong. I wasn't just like her. We were not two peas in a pod. I stood as still as I could so she'd relax her grip. "Okay . . . okay . . . I . . . I think I saw Rose Tulip in the bathroom cabinet."

"Well, that's better," she said, all perky. She let go and headed down the hall.

I quietly took Owen's hand and pulled him back toward the door. Then I pushed it open and we flew down the steps.

"Run, Owen, run fast!" I said, tugging him along beside me into the murky grove.

We were halfway through the trees when we heard Skyla's voice. "I know you can hear me, Naomi. You're going with me, one way or another!"

a flight of swallows

Out of breath, Owen and I spilled into Fabiola's living room. She and Gram looked up from the wedding gown that they were stuffing with tissue and wrapping in plastic.

"What's happened?" asked Gram.

I burst into tears, and Owen talked so fast I could barely understand him.

"She's coming and she's going to take Naomi away and she *hit* Naomi and she's going to hurt you!"

Gram hurried to me and examined my cheek, her mouth set in a straight line and something fierce building in her eyes. "You and Owen go out to the shed. Send Bernardo in here. You stay there and don't come out until I come to get you."

As we ran to the shed, I heard Skyla's muffled voice calling from the other side of the dark trees. "Nao-mee."

In the shed Bernardo stood in a half circle of wood shavings from the plank he had been planing. Owen's words tripped over each other when he explained about

Skyla. Bernardo quickly turned off the dangling lightbulb, and before he pulled the door shut on his way to the yard, he grabbed his biggest shovel.

I could smell the freshly shorn wood. I ran my fingers along the rippled aluminum wall.

"What's going to happen?" whispered Owen.

"I think she's going to come over and try to convince Gram to send me with her," I whispered back.

I kept hearing Skyla's words, "Something could happen to her any time now, old as she is."

Softly, Owen said, "Why doesn't Skyla want me, too?"

My mind tumbled to think of some comfort words. "It's plain and clear she only wants me so I can be friends with Clive's daughter and so she can get money from the state. So, I'm nothing special." I touched my cheek and winced from the tenderness. I could still hear Skyla saying that there was more where that came from.

Owen thought on what I'd said for a minute. Even in the almost dark, I could see his round eyes intent on my face. He shook his head. "I think she never wanted me when I was a baby because I wasn't . . . you know, like everyone else, and I think she doesn't want me now."

"But Gram wanted us, Owen. And our father. Those are the good things. We were lucky for that." I scooted over close to him and put my arm around his shoulders while we waited.

We heard Lulu's barking first. Owen and I carefully peeked through the window in the door. We could see Gram and Fabiola, who was now holding Lulu, and Bernardo by their side. The three stood shoulder to shoulder, like a barricade.

Skyla stood in front of them talking so soft, almost cooing, that we couldn't hear her words.

But Gram's voice carried in the crisp night air. "She is not going anywhere with you and that is that!"

The cooing stopped and Skyla's voice fired up. "Clive told me you'd be like this. If you don't go along, all I have to do is show up with a police officer. You can't prove any legal rights to her. She'll have to go with me. Is that what you want? Me showing up with a police officer to take Naomi?"

I held my stomach, thinking I might be sick. Would Gram have to let me go?

"Skyla, I'd go to the end of the earth to protect that child. I'll go to court if that's what I have to do."

Skyla laughed. "The court would never deny custody to a natural parent. Clive told me all about it. There's not a judge that wouldn't give me my own child."

"You abandoned those children!" said Gram. "That will count for something. And there's another kettle of fish to consider. What about their father?"

"Him? What about him? He hasn't seen them in years. He doesn't care." Skyla stumbled, then steadied herself. "Now where is she?"

"Skyla, what makes you think I'd turn her over, especially with you in your condition. You're drinking. I can tell."

"That does not concern you! Now, I'm saying it again. Clive, Naomi, and I are *going* to Las Vegas. Where is she?"

Bernardo took a few steps toward Skyla with the shovel pointed out.

Skyla walked backward, slowly, and waved a shaky finger at Gram. "Fine! I'll be back with Clive to pick up Naomi at noon on Saturday, and I expect her bags to be packed. If she's not ready, I'm going straight to the police. I'm not going to forget you making problems for me and Clive. Naomi doesn't belong to you. She belongs to me. She is *my* daughter."

Fabiola and Lulu spent the night with us in Baby Beluga, but it was a small comfort because I didn't sleep a straight ten minutes. I had ideas of Skyla and Clive scooping me up at any moment to the point I was more tired when I woke up Friday morning than when I'd gone to bed the night before. It didn't matter. We didn't go to school anyway, which was fine by me. I stuck to Gram like an ivy plant on the side of a barn and glanced over my shoulder at the least little sound. That afternoon, Gram went with Fabiola to do private errands and said I couldn't come along. Owen and I stayed with Bernardo, and Lulu was close by as guard dog. But even then, when one of the grove workers knocked on the door, I ran to the kitchen and started to cry.

That night Gram and Fabiola barely watched *Wheel of Fortune*. They had their heads together, talking quietlike the whole time. When I crawled into bed my body collapsed into the mattress, heavy and limp, like a half-full flour sack. It was a different kind of tired than I'd ever known my whole life.

Gram came to tuck me in, smiling.

I had already asked her a dozen times, but I had to ask again, "Are you sure Skyla's not coming for me tomorrow?"

"Don't you worry," said Gram. "Tomorrow you are definitely not going to be with Skyla."

"But the police —"

"Shush," said Gram. "I have plans, Naomi, but you don't need to be concerned with them. Now, can you muster a tiny smile for me? The last few days you've had a permanent wrinkled brow."

I struggled to make my mouth turn up on the ends. Then I skipped into sleep.

A regular sound, like a clock, rocked me in a deep, gentle fog with no nightmares *or* dreams, just nothingness, over and over. Mist and motion, mist and motion. I felt suspended in a hammock of sleep, swaying back and forth. When I did wake in the morning, I felt as peaceful as a kitten after a long nap, until I blinked several times. Then the restfulness startled out of me.

I sat up. "Owen!"

Sleepy eyed, Owen sat up and looked at me.

We both grabbed the sides of our beds.

The walls pitched and vibrated. An earthquake!

"Gram!" I called, but there was no answer.

I tried to think. What did they tell us to do in school? Stand in a doorway or a small bathroom.

I struggled to get out of bed and to help Owen. I pulled him along behind me and tried to balance with one hand against the trailer wall, but I could hardly stay straight. The shaking kept up at a steady pace.

"Gram!" I called again.

I stumbled down the narrow hallway with Owen. For a second I was afraid to look into the living room/kitchen. I'd seen those earthquake movies and the reports on television. Nothing left on the walls. Cupboards open and dishes smashed on the floor. I leaned forward and peeked into the room.

Gram and Fabiola sat at the drop-down table drinking coffee. Out the window behind them, cars sprinted by in the opposite direction. It wasn't an earthquake. Baby Beluga was moving down a highway!

Through the window in the front of the trailer, I could see Bernardo's truck towing us with his trailer hitch. Lulu was perched next to his shoulder on the top of the seat, looking out the back windshield at us and panting. Luggage and boxes snuggled tight in the truck bed, tied in with rope. My eyes shifted to the counters inside Baby Beluga.

They were stacked with boxes of groceries, bottled water, a twenty-four pack of Nature's Pure White bar soap, and an economy box of transparent tape.

I'd never seen Owen so happy. He jumped up and down the best he could, seeing how we were in a moving vehicle. He was giggling so hard he finally had to sit on the floor.

"Can Lulu ride back here with us?" he asked between fits of clapping.

"No," said Gram. "We are all moving into the safety of the truck as soon as Bernardo stops."

"Gram?" I said, still holding on to the side of the trailer for balance.

"Naomi, in my wildest dreams I never thought I'd up-root Baby Beluga. I told Skyla I'd go to the end of the earth to protect you, and I am fulfilling that prophecy. Besides, I always said you and Owen should know your Mexican history, so we are taking a holiday vacation to Mexico."

"To Oaxaca," said Fabiola, "to see our family and for *La*

Navidad, Christmas." Fabiola said this as if it was something we had planned, like a regular event on the calendar that we never missed. She held up a big driving map of Mexico. A red marker lined our route.

"Lemon Tree is close to here." She pointed near Tijuana, which bordered San Diego. Then she unfolded the map full size. "And we are going . . . here." Fabiola tapped her finger on a state in Mexico that was almost near Central America. We might as well be driving to New York City for how far away we were headed.

I took a step closer. Across the state were the letters *O A X A C A.* Pointing at them, I asked, "What does that mean?"

Fabiola laughed. "It is the name of the state. It's pronounced Wah-*hah*-kah. And here, at this star, is Oaxaca City, the capital of the state and the town where our family lives. They are very excited that we are coming. We have not seen them in too many years."

"But what about school?" asked Owen.

"Your winter break would have started the week after

next anyway and you don't start up again until January eighth. You're just missing an extra two weeks," said Gram.

"Yippee!" cried Owen.

"I already called and left messages for your teachers," said Gram. "Mrs. Maloney's going to collect our mail, water the plants, and feed Fabiola's chickens."

I wished I could have told Blanca that we were leaving. She would have loved to know that I was on my way to Mexico. What if her mom got promoted to another Value-City before we got back? Would I see her again?

I crossed the trailer and scooted in next to Gram. She put her arm around me. I looked out the window at the brown hills.

"We are on the lam," Gram said, "and for good reason. Yesterday, I met a nice young lady lawyer who had plenty to tell me. I got temporary guardianship of you and Owen. See this folder?" Gram held up a thick envelope. "I've got your birth certificates and my notarized papers right here." Gram glanced at Fabiola as if there was a secret passing between them. "We have a court hearing the day before you go back to school, January seventh. Come to find out, we have a free Legal Aid office for folks like me right in Lemon Tree. And we have Clive to thank for giving me the idea. I just wish I'd known about such a thing sooner."

"Does Skyla know?"

"She will as soon as she gets the notice. She's going to pitch a fit when she finds out. Naomi, I am taking a chance by going to court and letting a judge decide on us, and I could be opening another can of worms, but I don't see any other way."

I scrunched up my forehead. "But what if the judge says —"

"Do not even think that," said Gram. "The lawyer said the court would appoint a mediator, someone who isn't for one side or the other, to interview everyone involved, which means we will all get to answer. And on top of that, we're going to try and find your father and ask him to help us. The lawyer said the judge would weigh his wishes very heavily. He still has rights to you, too. If I can convince him to write a letter on our behalf . . . well, he's our ticket,

Naomi. And we *are* going to find him. We just have to believe it. . . ." Her voice dwindled into a sigh.

I wanted to believe it. I did.

"Do you know where he . . . our father . . . lives?"

"The last I knew, he lived in Puerto Escondido, near the ocean. The only thing I know for sure is that he comes to Oaxaca City every year for a few days before Christmas for that radish-carving festival on the twenty-third."

"What if he won't help us?"

"Santiago was always a good, kind man," said Gram. "I have to believe that he hasn't changed and wants the best for you. I am . . . I am . . . locked on the prospect of finding him."

Sitting so close, I could see dark puddles in the withered skin beneath Gram's eyes. Her hair had not been fluffed, and she looked smaller and older and more tired than I ever remembered. I suddenly wanted to scoop her up and rock her like a baby. I looked at Fabiola, studying the map, and I could see the back of Bernardo's head in the truck. I knew they hadn't been planning this trip. I turned to the window. A hundred birds sat on a telephone line, and in one instant they released and lifted with stubborn determination, trailing across the sky toward somewhere.

I patted Gram's hand, then reached across the table for my notebook. Turning to a clean page, I wrote a hundred times, *We will find him. We will find him. We will find him.* . . .

a passel of todays

Mexico paraded outside the cab of Bernardo's truck, but at times the scenery blurred and my mind clouded with all that had happened: The night when Skyla waltzed into Baby Beluga, the perfect M of her lips, me sitting on the floor while she braided my hair, Owen's face when he saw the bike, and my new clothes. My thoughts were also smudged with Thanksgiving Day, teachers' conferences, Children's Hospital, and the sting of Skyla's fury. Now, I was chasing a father who was nothing more than a wisp of smoke floating in the air, someone I didn't know for sure I would ever really touch.

Even though my life was a fog of the good and the bad, one thing was clear as a vinegar-shined window in my mind. I belonged with Gram and Owen. I wanted no part of living with Skyla, Clive, and Sapphire. If finding my father was my only hope, then I was going to latch on to every positive, forward-thinking, universe-tilting notion to fulfill that prophecy.

I just wished I didn't have all of Mexico standing between me and a sunshiny day.

12 a drey of squirrels

It was only five-thirty in the morning, but Bernardo wanted to arrive in Oaxaca City before the streets filled with workday traffic, so the truck and trailer already lumbered on the road. We had two hours of driving left.

In the dim early-morning light, Gram studied the tiny calendar on the back of her checkbook. "It's been four weeks since Skyla arrived in Lemon Tree. I feel like I've lived a year since that day and added a few hundred gray hairs. If someone had told me then that today we'd all be traveling in Mexico and staying in motels with Baby Beluga only spitting distance away, I would have more likely believed a cow jumped over the moon. Owen, settle down back there. You're as antsy as Lulu."

During the four days of the drive, Owen and I had spent time playing cards and that game where you call out the states from people's license plates. (I had no idea there were so many people from the United States in Mexico!) When we weren't playing games, Owen arranged blankets on the seat around himself, like a nest, and read out loud to Lulu. At night, we stopped at small motels. Bernardo and Owen slept in Baby Beluga with Lulu. Gram, Fabiola, and I slept inside the motel room. Now, as the truck and trailer motored around gentle curves of green hills, Owen bounced on the seat.

"Why don't you read to Lulu some more," I said.

"I don't feel like it," he said. "How much longer?"

Gram turned around, giving me a helpless look that told me her patience was wearing thin.

"Owen," I said. "Want to see my brand-spanking-new list?"

"Which one?"

I flipped through my notebook. I passed over the most recent list of "Regular and Everyday Worries about Mexico," which was based on everything I'd heard on the playground: stories about college kids who went to Tijuana, got thrown in jail for absolutely no reason, and were ransomed back to their parents for thousands of dollars; reports about people who went camping on the beach in

Baja and were murdered; warnings about drinking the water or eating the meat because it gave people horrible sicknesses; rumors that everyone peed on the side of the road so the whole country smelled.

When I turned to "Things I Saw on My Way to Oaxaca," I read aloud: "1) Lots of brown desert, 2) Cows, 3) Honking cars that wanted Baby Beluga out of their way, 4) Reddish hills but some green, 5) Cornfields, 6) Apple trees, 7) Burros grazing, 8) Bamboo forests, 9) Avocado trees, just like at home, 10) Green mountains with misty clouds around the tops."

"You forgot the dead dog on the side of the road and the squirrels all together under that tree," said Owen.

I wrote it down.

"And that lady selling tortillas at the gas station. And the spider that looked like a real scorpion but wasn't that got into Baby Beluga the first night . . . and you forgot the rainbow . . . oh, and the cockroaches at the little pink motel. Don't forget the cockroaches. . . ."

Slowly the truck climbed for over an hour with

occasional bursts of memory from Owen. Finally, in the distance, I saw a flat valley scattered with thousands of white rooftops.

"That is the city," said Bernardo. "It is on a mesa, a tabletop."

The low hills around the edges of the mesa reminded me of an old piece of copper pipe — green, gold, and rust-colored. Behind the foothills, on the horizon, giant curvy purple mountains stood guard. Below, the shadows of the wispy clouds overhead made the entire valley look mottled, like a camouflage jacket.

"Oh, my! I never dreamed I'd be in such a tropical place," said Gram.

I added *tropical* to my "Splendid Words" page.

"It is so good to be close to our home," said Fabiola, looking out the window, starry eyed.

Bernardo drove the truck down into the flatland next to dry brown fields that looked like they needed a deep soaking with a sprinkler.

"We are almost there," said Bernardo. "We are almost at Barrio Jalatlaco."

"I thought we were going to Oaxaca," Owen said.

"We are. *Barrio* means 'neighborhood,'" said Bernardo. "Hah-laht-*lah*-coe is the name of our neighborhood."

Gram, Owen, and I practiced the name by saying a lot of la-la-lahs and we made Bernardo laugh at our attempts.

As we got closer to the town, the streets became narrow and bumpy because the ground was set with stones in cement. Baby Beluga took up more than half the road. When another car came toward us, the driver had to pull up on the sidewalk to get by, but the driver wasn't mad. He just waved to us and smiled.

I read the street names that were printed on the sides of buildings, trying to pronounce them out loud, *"El Calvario, Refugio, Niños Heroes."*

Gram laughed. "We are not in Lemon Tree anymore."

"Here is the street," said Fabiola.

Bernardo turned down what looked like a long alley.

I sat up tall in the seat and stared out the truck window. I couldn't see any houses. Only walls and more walls, some of them two stories high. On both sides of the street were lengths of wooden fence, then brick walls, then cement walls, all painted different colors, but all run together. Black grills covered windows and doors that faced the street, and there didn't seem to be any roofs. Every now and then we passed big double wooden gates. What was behind them? Did my father live here? And where would Bernardo ever fit Baby Beluga?

Bernardo finally stopped in front of two rickety wooden gates that were taller than the truck. They hung crooked and barely met in the middle. He hopped out of the truck, unhitched the rope loop that held the gates together, and swung them open.

Behind them, a little world appeared in a grassy field with a giant tree, blooming purple, right in the middle.

"Will you look at that!" said Gram. "That's the biggest jacaranda I've ever seen."

A tiny gray house, square and squat, sat toward the

back of the lot. On one side of the house a huge full-grown vegetable garden sprawled over the dirt with a maverick vine overtaking the fence. On the other, a washing machine hugged the side of the house. Plastic clothespins shimmered in the morning sun, gripping four rows of laundry, already stiff from the dry air. Behind the house a bougainvillea spilled over from a neighbor's high back wall. Tiny walking paths crossed the yard, but it wasn't formal, like in a magazine. It was homey, like a trailer park.

Fabiola, Owen, Gram, and I slid off the truck seats and into the bumpy street.

"I don't think I've ever seen a cobblestone street," said Gram.

"They are everywhere here," said Fabiola. "You are lucky you have comfortable shoes. They are not easy on the feet."

Bernardo got back in the truck and began slowly backing the trailer into the narrow opening between the gates and, finally, parking it on the side of the house. Then he signaled for us to come, and he shut the big gates.

I could not take my eyes off the little house and the walls that surrounded it. An entire universe existed in this yard, but no one would know it from the street. Skyla and Clive would never find us here.

"*¡Hola! ¡Aquí estamos!* We are here," hollered Bernardo.

The screen door swung open and a man, two women, and a little boy came out.

Hugs, kisses, and pats on the back passed among the relatives. Bernardo and Fabiola introduced us. The house belonged to Fabiola's sister, Flora, and her husband, Pedro.

Flora and Fabiola looked alike except for two things. Fabiola had short, curly brown hair due to her permanent wave and wore tiny dot earrings, and Flora had short, straight brown hair and wore dangly earrings. Pedro reminded me of Santa Claus because of his gray mustache and his round belly that really did jiggle when he walked.

Graciela, their daughter, looked to be a little older than Skyla. She had the longest, thickest black hair I'd ever seen. It was perfectly straight and pulled back, half up, half down. If my bangs ever grew out, that was exactly how I would wear my hair. Her uniform of pink drawstring pants, a bunny-printed smock, and white tennis shoes made her look like a nurse at Children's Hospital, only she wasn't. Fabiola had already told us she was a doctor's assistant and helped with the well baby checkups at the clinic. She lived in the house, too, with her seven-year-old son, Rubén, who had cute pudgy cheeks. I already felt sorry for him because they were the kind that ladies love to pinch.

Everyone knew we did not speak Spanish, but they were all smiling at us. Flora and Graciela hugged us right off even though we didn't know one another yet.

"I speak English," said Graciela, smiling at me. "And my parents, they speak a little bit."

I smiled back at her.

Rubén walked over to Owen. His hair was black and cut short in a grown-up haircut. Someone had taken some time to part it perfect on the side and comb it down slick with gel. Even though it was almost Christmas, it was hot here so he wore shorts and sandals. He pulled a small rubber ball out of his pocket and held it up.

Owen nodded and they ran over to the side yard and began tossing the ball back and forth.

Gram shook her head and said, "Give a boy a ball and that's all it takes to seal international relations."

I followed everyone else into the house, peeking in rooms as we headed toward the kitchen at the very back. The house had only two bedrooms, a living room, a bathroom, and a kitchen. Baby Beluga was almost as big. Some of the windows didn't have screens and were open to the world. By the looks of all the iron chairs on the lawn, I guessed the outside was part of their living area, too, just like at Avocado Acres.

The aroma of something cooking tickled my nose. In the kitchen Flora pointed for us to sit down at the long table that was covered with a plastic flowered tablecloth. Fabiola poured Gram and me cups of juice. It tasted like a punch but with cinnamon. I couldn't decide if I liked it or not. Before we knew it, Flora was serving up eggs, tortillas, and spicy sausage. Graciela called Owen and Rubén in from outside and everyone crowded around the table.

During breakfast Bernardo and Fabiola told the story of what happened to us. I could tell because their sentences were filled with our names as well as Skyla's and Clive's.

Flora, who was still standing at the stove with a wooden spatula in the air, said, "León . . . León. . . ." She started talking fast to Fabiola.

"She says that the cheese lady at the market married a León," said Fabiola. "Tomorrow, when we shop for dinner, we will talk to her."

Gram's face scrunched up in worry. "But isn't León a common name?"

"Yes and no," said Fabiola. "There are many with the name, but it is an old name with much history and, well, cousins know other cousins and other cousins know more."

"Maybe we'll be lucky," I said.

"Maybe," said Gram, but I could tell that suddenly she wasn't convinced. What had happened to her true feelings about thinking positive?

From what I could figure with Fabiola and Graciela translating every few sentences, the rest of the talk was everyone catching up on their personal family news. I looked around the kitchen at the odd things on the walls: a colorful peacock painted on some strange paper that looked like a leathery bag, little ceramic plates with fruits and vegetables painted on them, a line of tiny tin mirrors painted with pink and red flowers, and a picture of a beautiful queen, in a long robe decorated with gold and pearls, wearing a crown on her head.

Graciela noticed me staring at the picture. "*Nuestra Señora de la Soledad.* Our Lady of Solitude," she said, "the patron saint of Oaxaca. You can see the statue in *la basílica,* a beautiful old church not too far from *el zócalo,* the town square."

"Soledad. That's my middle name. And Owen's, too."

"It is a very special name in Oaxaca," said Graciela.

I smiled at her, thinking that it must have been special for my father, too.

By the time we finished eating breakfast it was only eight-thirty in the morning, but it felt like noon. Pedro left for work at a big hotel where he was a gardener and

Graciela left for the clinic. Owen and Rubén went out to Flora's garden. Bernardo pointed out a giant spider on the fence and told them never to kill that particular type because they were considered very good luck in Oaxaca. The boys then set out on a "lucky spider" hunt.

I helped Gram set up housekeeping in Baby Beluga. First we opened all the windows. Then Gram unlocked the storage bay and pulled out a long piece of green indoor-outdoor carpet and Mrs. Maloney's card table and chairs.

"She loaned them to me in my time of need," said Gram. "Wasn't that nice?"

I had to smile, thinking of Mrs. Maloney and Gram conspiring to bring us to Mexico. I unrolled the blue awning, propping it up with poles that had been tied to the side of the trailer. This made a nice shady spot. As we arranged the table and chairs, Gram hummed the whole while.

When everything was positioned, Gram put her hands on her hips and said, "Naomi, I believe I feel like a clean, fluffed sheet on bed-making day. Yes . . . I think that's how I feel."

I heard a tickle of hesitation in Gram's voice as if she was trying to convince herself of her own cheerfulness, but even so, she did continue with her humming.

Bernardo sat under the jacaranda tree with a panel of wood and his tools. I went inside and found the twenty-four pack of Nature's Pure White, unwrapped one of the bars, then joined him.

"It is nice here, yes?" said Bernardo, handing me a small knife.

I nodded.

"Tomorrow my cousin Beni, he is coming for dinner and you will meet him. We are carving together this year in the festival with Pedro. It will be in *el zócalo,* the square in the middle of town, in only . . . twelve days. We must decide on our presentation soon."

"That's plenty of time, right?" I said.

Bernardo adjusted his straw hat. "Some people spend many months deciding on a presentation. Plus it is not a long time when relatives must agree." He nodded toward my carving. "What is inside?"

I wished I could look into the soap and say, "It is my father inside." Then I could just carve away and find his face staring at me. Wouldn't that be easy? What would Bernardo think if I told him my silly thoughts?

I held up the bar against the turquoise sky and examined it. "Maybe a squirrel, sitting up, with the tail like this." I waved my hand, making the S shape. "What will you paint?"

"Maybe a sunrise over the mountains," he said. "But we will see what happens. Oaxaca, she is a city of magic and surprises. When I am here, I am different, so the art is different."

A gentle breeze tickled my face with warm air. I looked around at the walls that sheltered me and took a deep breath, but it was not the worrisome kind. It was the relief kind.

I swept my knife across the soap and tiny shavings darted and swirled in the air. As I watched the white pirouettes, my own laughter startled me.

13
a sleuth of bears

"Naomi, are you going with us?" called Gram.

I stood behind a giant zucchini plant with Owen and Rubén, gawking at the garden spider that was as big as my hand.

"Coming!" I said, quickly leaving the boys to their treasure and hurrying to join Fabiola, Flora, and Gram, who were already at the front gate. I didn't want to miss meeting the cheese lady.

We walked through the uneven streets of Barrio Jalatlaco to *el mercado,* the market. Even though they were out in the neighborhood, Fabiola and Flora still wore long bib aprons over their clothes. (Gram had not deviated from her pantsuit and running shoes.) They all carried big mesh bags for the groceries. I hugged my notebook, wanting it handy in case I was lucky enough to make another entry to my newest page: "Everything We Know About Our Father": 1) His name is Santiago Zamora León. We know this for sure because Gram dug out our birth certificates, 2) Santiago Zamora is also the name of a town in Guatemala, but Fabiola said it is only a coincidence, 3) He lives in Puerto Escondido near the ocean in the state of Oaxaca. *Puerto Escondido* means "hidden port" in Spanish, 4) Puerto Escondido is a long way from Oaxaca City, maybe five hours driving, 5) He is a fisherman and has a boat, 6) He is a carver, 7) In Gram's eyes he was always a good, kind man, 8) Once, he wanted us.

After five blocks we reached a building that looked like a big white warehouse. On the front, giant red letters formed the words *Mercado de la Merced*. I expected a grocery store or a supermarket, but this was different from any I had ever seen. Inside, stalls and tables crowded the cement-floor room. It was a party of colors and smells: flowers, tortillas, packages of fireworks, piñatas, fruit, raw meat, herbs and vegetables, ground spices in big canning jars. An entire table of different types of chiles towered as high as my shoulders. I smelled strawberries and oranges from the fruit juice stand. A woman sat on the floor next to a big steaming pot and sold tamales while she nursed her baby.

We found the cheese lady balanced on a high stool behind the counter with small wheels of white cheese stacked up around her. Behind her on the wall, a sign read, "*Quesillo.*"

"Keh-sill-owe," I said, sounding out the word.

Flora and Fabiola nodded approvingly.

"It's pronounced keh-*see*-owe," said Fabiola. "But you are learning very fast, Naomi."

The woman pulled long two-inch-wide strips from the cheese wheels and wrapped them into giant balls. Flora pointed to one and the lady weighed it on a scale, then expertly packaged it in white paper and handed it over. Fabiola and Flora began visiting with her and I heard the name Santiago León.

I studied the woman's face for recognition. Was she a relative? Did she know my father? Would she know how to find him? I gazed up at her, hoping, as if she was a queen about to tell me my destiny.

The lady looked at me, smiled, and handed me a strip of cheese.

"She married a León," said Fabiola. "She has not heard of your father, but her husband has many cousins she has not met and some live near the ocean. She will ask the family tonight and will call if she finds out anything."

Flora was already writing her number on a piece of paper and handing it through the stacks of cheese wheels. I waved at the lady before we turned away.

The strip of cheese was similar to the string cheese that Gram used to buy in Lemon Tree at the supermarket, only creamier and softer. I decided that *quesillo* was my new favorite food in Mexico. I flipped through my notebook and started a new list, "Superb Spanish Words": 1) *Jalatlaco,* 2) *Mercado,* 3) *Quesillo.* Later I added 4) *Mole,* the type of sauce on the tamale we ate on *el mercado* patio, and 5) *Piña, coco,* the pineapple/coconut ice cream I licked all the way home.

That night Bernardo's cousin Beni came for dinner. He was as short as Bernardo but much younger and seemed more like a son than a cousin. He entertained us by making silly faces at Rubén and Owen, which sent them into fits of giggles. Bernardo had brought some of my carvings inside for the centerpiece on the dinner table. Beni carefully examined them. "Very good," he said.

Every time the phone rang, I thought about the cheese lady. Had she arrived home from work yet? Did she ask her husband if he knew my father? So far the only calls had been for Graciela.

Everyone seemed to talk at the same time during dinner. Spanish songs hummed on the radio in the background and food platters rocked gently from hand to hand. I concentrated on the chicken with red gravy that was very spicy. Fabiola had made quesadillas, too, from big flour tortillas folded in half. Inside, *el quesillo* melted over yellow squash blossoms. I ate every bite. This was a far cry from Thursday pork chops!

When dinner was over, everyone stayed at the table and drank coffee and hot chocolate while we talked about the radish competition. Fabiola translated.

"Let's do a traditional scene — a church or a Nativity," said Pedro.

Beni shook his head. "We did that last year and we did not even place in the top five." He pulled out some papers from his pocket and unfolded them. He held up the first sketch, a scene with spaceships and aliens.

"No, no, no," groaned Bernardo and Pedro.

The next was a drawing of a marching band.

More groans.

Then a church.

"Everyone does *la catedral*," said Flora, shaking her head.

They argued, their voices growing louder.

Beni slammed his fist on the table and then got up and walked outside. Bernardo and Pedro shrugged their shoulders and threw their arms in the air.

"Why are they so angry?" Gram asked.

"Because they wish to create something different this year — something that will catch the eyes of the judges. They all have their own ideas and they are all stubborn.

They must decide on their presentation soon. The radishes are delivered from the fields next week. Then they have only three days left to carve."

In five minutes Beni was back and the men pored over the sketches again. I thought it was funny that he got mad and then came back and pretended there hadn't been a cross word between them.

The phone rang and when Flora answered it, she glanced at me.

I crossed my fingers for luck. Please let it be good news.

After a short conversation Flora hung up and reported to Fabiola.

"The woman we met today," said Fabiola, "her husband has no relatives named Santiago León, who live in Puerto Escondido. I am sorry."

Gram's shoulders sagged a little.

"Couldn't we try the phone book?" I said.

"Naomi, I thought of that, and there are four pages of Leóns and no Santiagos," said Gram, wearing her disappointment. "If it's our last resort I'll try it, but we might as well look for a needle in a haystack."

"We can't give up," I said. "What about Bernardo's friends? Remember? The ones who brought our father to Lemon Tree when he met Skyla."

Bernardo looked at me sadly. "No, no, Naomi. Those men have not lived here for many years. But the carving community is very knowing about the business of each other. On *La Noche de los Rábanos*, hopefully someone will know something about Santiago León."

"See," I said, looking at Gram.

"Well, let's hope that works out because if he doesn't show up at that festival, we won't have time to go on a wild-goose chase to another part of the state."

What was the matter with Gram? What happened to all her self-prophecy talk and planting sunshine in our brains? Had she forgotten what could happen to me if we didn't find my father?

The next day before breakfast, Gram called Mrs. Maloney from Flora's phone to check on things.

"Skyla and Clive came back to Avocado Acres from Las Vegas," she reported to me and Owen as we sat in Baby Beluga. "They had Clive's daughter with them. I guess she is a sad-faced thing. Skyla had already received copies of my temporary guardianship papers and was none too happy. When she found us gone, she marched over to Mrs. Maloney's to play twenty questions about where we were and when we'd be back. That sweet old thing just told them we'd gone on a little holiday vacation."

"What did they do?" I asked.

"They traipsed through the grove to Fabiola and Bernardo's and found them gone, too. Mrs. Maloney watched them come back and get into the car. Then they left. Only there's something I didn't think about before we took off. It might be nothing . . . but Skyla knows about this festival that Santiago comes to every year. And she knows that Fabiola and Bernardo are from this same town.

It wouldn't be hard for her to put two and two together about where we might have gone."

"Would she come here?" asked Owen.

"No . . . she would have no reason to come. Technically she can't touch you until the judge makes a decision," said Gram, looking at us and wringing her hands. "But . . . according to the fine print on the guardianship papers, I probably wasn't supposed to take you out of the country. If Skyla suspects and could prove that I did, by letting the authorities know or hiring an investigator . . . well . . . it wouldn't look good to the mediator or the judge."

"Gram!" I whined, not believing what I'd heard. Why hadn't she warned us about all this before?

"Maybe I'm letting my imagination run pell-mell. I just wouldn't put anything past Skyla at this point."

I didn't want to take the chance that Gram's imagination was right. I wanted to find my father and the sooner, the better.

I hadn't been able to forget about the phone book. I asked Graciela how to say, "I am looking for Santiago León" in Spanish. It was simple. *"Busco a Santiago León."* I wrote it in my notebook. She didn't seem to suspect anything, and after she and Pedro left for work and Flora, Fabiola, and Gram left to do the daily marketing, I told Owen what I wanted to do.

"Somebody has to know him or be related to him. But you have to keep this a secret, okay?"

"Why?"

"I don't want Gram putting a stop to it because she doesn't want us imposing on Flora's phone. Or because she doesn't want us talking to strangers. Or because she doesn't want us bothering folks with unnecessary calls. You know how particular she can be."

"Can Rubén help?" asked Owen.

"Yes, but he can't tell. Can you make him understand?"

Rubén understood. We made a system. Owen read off the number from the phone book. I dialed and asked for Santiago León. A lot of people hung up immediately or said, "No, no." If I shook my head, Rubén crossed the number off the list. If the person on the other end of the line said anything other than no, I handed the phone to Rubén to talk to them in Spanish. Sometimes Rubén had a long conversation with people he didn't know and gave out his name and number. I was sure Gram would not approve.

When we heard Flora, Fabiola, and Gram come through the gate, we closed the phone book.

"¿Mañana?" asked Rubén.

"Yes, tomorrow, we'll try again mañana," I said, tapping my finger to my mouth to remind him and Owen to keep quiet.

The next morning Rubén became more animated in his telephone conversations, and occasionally I heard our names thrown in as well. What was he telling these strangers? We made slow progress through the phone book, but at least I felt that by saying our father's name over and over, it was somehow bringing us closer to him. We still had nine days until the festival.

Again, as soon as we heard the front gate and the

women's voices, we hung up the phone, the boys took off to play, and I grabbed my box of carvings and hurried to the table. I had been carving bears for the past few days. When Gram walked into the kitchen, I was buffing the most recent one with a towel.

"It looks like you've been busy," said Gram.

"Very busy," I said seriously as I added a cub to the long migration that crossed the table.

14   a leap of leopards

Church bells clanged, announcing Sunday mass, and as soon as they finished their long echo, the phone rang. Flora answered it and said, "Rubén?" She looked puzzled. I held my breath. Rubén was outside with Owen and, even though I probably wouldn't be able to talk to the person on the line, I still wanted to grab the receiver. Flora handed the phone to Graciela.

Graciela looked at Gram and me, also confused. "Rubén does not get calls." She took the phone and began talking. While she listened to the caller, she glanced at me.

I picked at my *pan dulce,* sweet breakfast bread, making a tiny pyramid of crusty pastry, praying it was news about my father.

Graciela reached for a pencil and paper and wrote down a message, thanked the caller, and hung up. She walked to the door and called Rubén and Owen. In a few minutes, the three of us sat on one side of the table facing Flora, Fabiola, Gram, and Graciela.

Owen and Rubén wiggled and squirmed, eager to get back outside to play, but I suspected, based on the way Graciela's arms were crossed, that this was not going to be a picnic.

"It seems my son and his new friends have been calling listings in the phone book and asking for Santiago León," said Graciela. "Someone they called yesterday told me that yes, they have discovered they are a cousin by marriage of Santiago's aunt Teresa. They spoke to Rubén for a long time yesterday. I have the number. That is the good news."

Owen and Rubén clapped their hands. I started to smile until I saw Graciela's serious face and raised eyebrows.

Here it came. Now, the bad.

"But the person who called lives in a neighborhood outside of the city. It's a toll call, which means it cost money for each minute." Graciela studied the paper, looking worried. "How many calls did you make outside of our area?"

I took a deep breath. "Probably lots."

"Naomi, I am surprised at you! You did that? Without permission?" said Gram.

I stared at my breadcrumb pyramid and bit my bottom lip. Didn't Gram want me to find my father?

Gram stared at Owen and me in disbelief. "You can be sure, Graciela, that I will pay for that phone bill and that these children will work off the error of their ways."

Flora said something to Rubén in Spanish and Rubén hung his head.

"I will call the number," said Graciela, turning back toward the phone.

I wasn't sure, but I thought I saw a tiny smile on Graciela's face.

The next morning, standing in front of the narrow mirror in Gram's bedroom, I admired the Mexican girl looking back at me. I wore a new white peasant blouse with puffed sleeves that Gram had bought at *el mercado*. I touched the gathered neckline and blue and yellow embroidery down the center front. Gram always said that clothes made the person, meaning that when a girl put on a wedding dress she felt like a bride, or if she put on a three-piece suit, she felt like a businessperson. I was beginning to think Gram was right because after completing my outfit with a pair of slide-in sandals called huaraches, I knew I fit in with all the other brown girls in the barrio. What would my father's aunt Teresa think of me?

After lunch Bernardo drove Gram, Fabiola, Owen, and me to another part of Oaxaca City. In the truck I straightened my new blouse a dozen times and again readjusted the headband that Graciela had loaned me. Owen played with the snap on the bottom of his new western-style shirt, the kind Rubén wore. Although not one person in Mexico had said a peep about his tape usage, the plaid pattern of the shirt did help matters by making the strips seem less noticeable. From the front seat, Gram looked back at us every few minutes. She had cooled some about the phone calls, but not until we had raked Flora's yard and pulled weeds all yesterday afternoon. She leaned forward to look out the front window at where we were headed, holding a cotton hanky she'd bought at *el mercado*. She'd already worried it into a twisted roll, which reminded me that she was hungry for information, too.

We drove past churches and parks with statues and fountains. Past open markets and men selling ice cream from wheeled pushcarts at street corners. More bumpy streets with big potholes bounced us on the seat. Finally we headed down a road that was nothing more than a dirt path lined with ramshackle fences. The size and condition of some of the houses made Baby Beluga look like a mansion.

The truck crawled in front of a chain-link fence that had been threaded with bamboo sticks.

"*¡Aquí! ¡Mira!*" said Bernardo.

"This is the address," said Fabiola.

We got out of the truck and Bernardo opened the gate.

The small wood house seemed to lean to the right, as if one side was shorter than the other. The yard was dirt with flowerbeds marked off by rocks arranged in circles.

Ceramic statues of saints decorated almost every flower-bed, along with small cement bowls filled with birdseed and old cooking pots filled with water.

A tiny woman came out of the house wearing a long flower-print skirt, tennis shoes with no laces, and a white blouse with pink embroidery. Her gray hair separated down the middle into two long braids.

Bernardo and Fabiola walked forward and spoke to the woman before bringing her to us. "This is your great-aunt Teresa," said Fabiola. "She speaks Zapotec and a little Spanish, and I speak Spanish and a little Zapotec. She says the parents of your father are no longer alive, and his brothers and sisters live in another part of the state."

The woman studied Owen and stroked his hair. Then she took my face in her hands and turned it from side to side. Her touch was as gentle as a silky blanket. She nodded and spoke to Fabiola.

"She says she can see the face of your father in your face," said Fabiola.

I looked at Teresa. I searched for my father's face in

hers. Did he have the same high cheeks, the same dark skin and dancing eyes?

Teresa went into the house and brought out orange drinks and cookies, and we all sat in plastic chairs under a tree. Every few minutes Fabiola gave a running update on the conversation.

"At one time your father's family grew corn. They carved when there was not much fieldwork. But now that the father of Santiago is no longer alive and his brothers have moved away, Santiago is the only one to continue the carving. It is tradition that the carvers participate in *La Noche de los Rábanos*. A León has entered the competition every year for over one hundred years."

"A hundred years?" I said. "That's amazing. Does Aunt Teresa come there, too?"

Fabiola asked. "She says no, that it is too many people and the festivities continue too late at night. Besides, she has work to do for Santiago and must finish before he arrives."

Teresa stood up and waved at us to follow her to the

backyard. She opened a door to a wooden shed and pointed inside.

On makeshift shelves of boards and bricks, a brigade of wood carvings appeared before us, painted in every bright color and decorated with fancy black lines and tiny dots: mermaids, tigers, roosters, Nativity scenes, serpents, birds of prey, dancing rabbits, cats, bugs, and lions.

"My father did these?" I asked, my eyes sweeping over the collection.

"*Alebrijes*," said Teresa, smiling and nodding.

"That's the Zapotec word for wood carvings," said Fabiola. "Sometimes we call them *animalitos*, little wooden animals. They are Santiago's. He brings them to her several times a year. It is the tradition that the men carve the *alebrijes* and the women paint them."

Teresa reached into her skirt pocket and handed an old photo to Bernardo, who handed it to me.

"Your father when he was a little boy," said Bernardo. "With his father."

Owen and I huddled over the photo. A happy boy

about ten years old held a wooden leopard and stood next to a man with a carving of a dog riding a bicycle. The boy had brown eyes, a mop of unruly brown hair, and milky brown skin.

"It looks just like you, Naomi!" said Owen.

Gram leaned over to see. "For heaven's sake. You're the spitting image of him at that age."

Even I could see it was true. Same hair, same eyes, same skin, same expression. I couldn't stop smiling.

Teresa patted me on the shoulder, and when I tried to return the photo she pressed it into my palm and closed my fingers around it.

As we walked to the front yard, Bernardo said, "There is something else. All the participants for the festival must register by December eighteenth at the municipal building. Pedro, Beni, and I, we already put our names on the papers."

"But he comes every year, right?" said Owen.

"According to Teresa, he only missed one year when he could not get through because the roads flooded," said

Fabiola. "A León cousin carved for the family in the contest that year. Teresa is convinced he will come this year, with the permission of God, of course. He usually arrives in time for *Las Posadas* because he loves very much to participate and they start tonight."

Graciela had already explained *Las Posadas* to me, how for nine nights before Christmas, neighborhoods held their own get-togethers, walking through the streets, knocking on doors and pretending to look for shelter, just like Mary and Joseph did in Bethlehem.

Today was the sixteenth. He'd have to be here within two days to register for the festival, and tonight his favorite celebration started. My stomach turned a cartwheel.

"Teresa will call some of her relatives so that maybe they can get a message to Santiago, but she worries that he is traveling already."

"*Gracias,*" I said, and gave her a quick hug.

On the way home in the truck, I stared at the photo in my hand of the smiling boy and his father. They were my family, who had come to this town year after year for one special occasion. I sat a little taller in my seat. No wonder Beni examined my carvings. I was from the León family, who had been carving in the festival for over a hundred years.

I pulled out my notebook and added to "Everything We Know About Our Father": 9) He loves *Las Posadas,* 10) I look just like him.

15   a piteousness of doves

Fabiola hung up the phone and shook her head and frowned. It had been three days since we'd been to Aunt Teresa's and still Santiago had not arrived. "Teresa, she feels confident that he still might come for the holidays. Possibly for the New Year. . . ."

"I will take Owen and Rubén to the municipal building and check the registration list this morning," said Bernardo.

"Well, I guess that is that," said Gram, looking into her plate of eggs.

"Gram, he still might come!" I scooted my chair away from the table and walked outside to the jacaranda tree and sat down.

Tonight was Barrio Jalatlaco's *posada,* and tomorrow the radishes would be delivered. Where was Santiago? What could have happened? He was going to miss everything, including us.

I stayed beneath the tree while Bernardo left with the boys, and Gram, Fabiola, and Flora left for *el mercado*.

A breeze lifted the loose purple jacaranda blossoms and sprinkled them over me. Picking up a bar of soap, I held it against the sky and imagined a little white dove inside. I rounded the corners of the bar and smoothed the arch that would be the back. I thought of Blanca. I wondered what she was doing and if she missed me. I thought about Mr. Marble and Ms. Morimoto. If I didn't find my father, would I have to live in Las Vegas and leave my life in Lemon Tree?

I worked and whittled, scraped and dug. But when I got to the center, there was nothing there, only the ground covered with my snowy frustrations.

I whispered to the leaves and the purple flowers, "Santiago, you don't have to be our father if you don't want to. Just show up and help me. Please?"

As I picked up another bar of soap to begin again, the gate opened and Owen walked toward me, with Rubén following. "It's okay, Naomi. It's okay."

Had Santiago registered at the municipal building?

But when Bernardo walked into the yard behind the boys and I saw his sad, soft-hearted eyes, I knew that Owen had only been trying to reassure me. There was no good news to give.

That night, before *Las Posadas,* Graciela brushed my hair until it shimmered like velvet. Since I'd been thinking so much about my father, I wondered about Rubén's. Gram would say to let it be and mind my own affairs. Blanca would tell me to ask lots of questions and get lots of answers.

"Graciela, *dónde está* Rubén's father?"

She stopped brushing.

I hoped I hadn't been too rude or nosy.

"We are no longer together."

"Did you ever want to leave Rubén with Flora and Pedro and go look for your life?"

Graciela turned me around to face her. She carefully

situated a beaded headband in my hair. "No, Naomi. You see, I am looking for my own life right here, *with* Rubén."

At eight, when the sky was filled with darkness, we all walked the few blocks through the barrio to a small hotel for *Las Posadas*. Many of the neighbors gathered there in the street, as well as tourists who were staying at the hotels. Flora and Pedro and Graciela seemed to know almost everyone. In just a matter of minutes, the road filled with people.

The door to the inn opened and a handsome man with black hair and a beard walked out into the street with his two teenage daughters, their arms full of baskets.

"Look," said Fabiola. "He has *las candelas,* the torches."

The father gave the adults the long sticks of bamboo with a candle stuck in the top surrounded by an upside-down cellophane umbrella.

One daughter handed me long wire sparklers, at least three feet long, then passed whistles to the youngest children. The other daughter gave firecrackers to the boys.

Owen held up a bundle of pink and white firecrackers to show me, grinning and jumping up and down. Rubén copied him.

The man and his daughters lit the wicks of *las candelas* and then everyone passed the flames, candle to candle, until the street glowed with soft lights. One of the older boys held a candle and the younger ones ran to it and lit their firecrackers, tossing them quickly away from the crowd.

Pop! Pop! Crack!

The huddle of people began walking slowly through the street. Every person, from the smallest to the oldest, held a sparkler, candle, or firecracker to light the night. I held my sparkler out and watched the tiny white pinpoints sprinkle onto the street. The sound of the firecrackers echoed off the stone streets and brick walls. People wove like a snake on the cobblestones, then stopped at the first door and started to sing.

"It is a famous song about this night," whispered Fabiola. "It says, 'The Queen of Heaven is asking for shelter for only one night under your roof.'"

On the other side of the door, someone answered them! I looked up at Fabiola, surprised.

She nodded. "The people wait behind the door. They said, '*No hay posada.* There is no shelter here.'"

"Watch," said Graciela. "The people who turned us away will come out of the house and join us."

As I peeked back through the crowd, the door opened and a man and a woman stepped out. Another neighbor passed them some candles, which they lit.

Then the parade started again. As I walked, my sparkler spilled a circle of brightness in front of me. Gram had a bamboo *candelero,* and when I glanced up at her in that light, her face looked soft and contented. She hummed along with the singers even though she didn't know the words.

The song continued and people's voices became stronger, floating upward and echoing off the walls of the barrio. At each house it was as if part of me knocked on the door, too, asking about my father and getting no answers.

Spurts of light and noise surrounded me. I felt tears

in my eyes and wiped away the drops on my lashes. We stopped at another door and the people's voices sang louder. Again, someone from behind the door called back to them.

"No hay posada."

The procession circled the block and stopped in front of the inn where we had begun. The father who had passed out *los candeleros* knocked on his own door and sang out the words of the song.

A woman's voice sang back.

Graciela whispered, "'Come in, holy pilgrims. Welcome to this place. Although this house is modest, our heart is big.'"

Everyone cheered loudly and the boys threw an army of firecrackers, the noise peppering the street. My tears spilled over.

Graciela hugged me. "It is a joy and a sadness in the heart at the same time, no?"

I nodded. No wonder my father loved *Las Posadas.* Then, as quickly as my tears had come, the mood around us changed. The doors flung open and several women came out with trays of sandwiches that Fabiola called *tortas*. The daughters served punch from a big pot.

On a nearby rooftop I noticed a boy swing a rope back and forth, then let go. Another boy on a rooftop on the other side of the street caught it, and as he pulled, a piñata slowly rose from the ground.

Someone held up a stick and the crowd clapped and cheered. Even the youngest children received a turn tapping the piñata. Owen swung and got a good crack. When everyone whooped for him, he bowed, and the people laughed, but not making fun, like in Lemon Tree. When the bigger boys took their turns and the piñata broke, Owen ran in with the rest and came back to me with his hands full of something that looked like short sticks of bamboo.

"Sugarcane," said Graciela. She took the thick cane, peeled back the top like a banana, and handed a piece to Owen and another to me. "Taste it."

Owen ran off with the sugarcane dangling from his mouth like a cigar. I carefully put the white bark to my lips and sucked on the sweetness.

One after the other, the pottery insides of the five piñatas clattered onto the street and little children ran to collect the peanuts, small oranges, and sugarcane that spilled from their clay tummies. The women passed out orange, pink, and yellow tissue-paper bundles to each person. Then people began to drift away, in twos and threes, back to their own parts of the neighborhood. As they left, they called out, "*¡Feliz Navidad!*"

We headed home, too. Flora, Gram, and Fabiola walked arm in arm ahead of me, three links in a chain. Bernardo and Pedro walked behind us, talking in their deep Spanish voices, probably about the radishes that would be delivered from the fields tomorrow. Rubén and Owen, on one side of me, already nibbled the cookies and candy that had been inside the tissue bundles. On the other side, Graciela held my hand. Every few minutes she looked down at me and smiled with a face full of kindness.

Just for a blink of my eye, I pretended that Graciela was my mother. I wondered if my father had ever married again. Maybe he would show up and he would meet

Graciela and they could get married. Then Owen, Gram, and I could live with them in a little house like Flora and Pedro's, with Fabiola and Bernardo close by. I would never have to go back to Lemon Tree and take the chance of having to live with Skyla. Every year we could all walk home from *Las Posadas* together, one big family.

We turned the corner and the street lamp gave off enough light so that we could see a lone figure up ahead standing in front of the wooden gates.

"I told Beni to come over so we can make the decisions tonight," said Bernardo.

Pedro waved and the person waved back.

As we walked closer, I thought, What if it isn't Beni? What if it's my father?

But it wasn't. It was Beni.

Everyone went to bed except for the men, who huddled together in the yard and discussed what they would carve for the festival. With my box of carvings under my arm, I tiptoed into Flora's kitchen for the last of the hot chocolate, which I knew was on the back of the stove. As I sipped, I examined a jacaranda branch that Rubén had dragged inside and left on Flora's table.

I picked up the branch and held it above my animals. I moved the branch back and forth like a puppeteer and imagined what my father had once carved for us. Then I held the branch upright, as if it grew out of the table. Since it was flat on the bottom, it balanced and stood like a young sapling. I braced it with Flora's salt and pepper shakers and bottles of hot sauce for extra support, then carefully began placing my soap figures among the spindly twigs.

Beni walked in, and while he drank a glass of water, he glanced at my arrangements on the table. He came closer, studying the animals in the tree.

"Don't touch. Don't touch," he said. Then he ran outside.

16 a team of horses

"¡Finalmente!" said Fabiola as I walked into the kitchen for breakfast. "They would not tell us what they decided to carve until you got here." She turned back to the stove to flip a tortilla on what Gram called the black trivet.

"We wait until everyone is here," said Bernardo.

Pedro winked at me.

"Here's the rest of us," said Gram, with Owen and Rubén right behind her.

My carvings were all over the table. Bernardo scooted his chair and pulled another chair over so I could sit between him and Pedro.

"¿Qué?" said Flora. "What? Tell us."

Bernardo started talking fast and excited in Spanish and Pedro nodded. Then Pedro stood up and paced around the kitchen, describing something and using his hands to express his excitement, waving them around. All this made his big belly dance.

Fabiola translated. "A gigantic branch like a big tree. Instead of leaves, there will be pigs and birds and fish and crocodiles. The panther lying here and an elephant sleeping there. Little parades. Giraffes and monkeys all together . . ."

Pedro sat back down and reached over and hugged my shoulder.

". . . and on the top," continued Fabiola, "*un león*, the king of beasts. It will be *maravilloso*, wonderful!" (I was definitely going to add *maravilloso* to the "Superb Spanish Words" list.)

"Shhh . . . shhh. . . . the neighbors . . . they could hear," said Pedro, putting his finger to his mustache. "People are jealous and could steal our ideas."

"Naomi, you can come to the market with me or stay and carve with these crazy men all day," said Graciela.

I knew she was kidding. "*Aquí,*" I said. "Here."

Graciela rolled her eyes. "*Bueno, como quieras.* As you wish." She pulled the shade on the back door before she walked out.

A few minutes later Beni arrived. He backed a truck into the yard and unloaded tubs filled with twisted and gnarled, knotty and contorted red vegetables that didn't resemble any delicate little radish that came from Gram's garden.

Gram stood over them with her hands on her hips. "I have never seen anything like them in my life. Why, they look like giant, overgrown yams that went through a pretzel maker. I think some of these are as tall as Owen."

Bernardo, Pedro, and Beni each dragged a big tub of radishes into Flora's kitchen.

Owen and Rubén had the job of misting the radishes with water so they would not dry out. They both took this duty seriously and sat on the floor with their water bottles ready, waiting for the first cuts to be made.

Bernardo grinned at me and rubbed his hands together in anticipation. Then he picked up a knife and started to carve.

"What happens to these radishes after the festival?" asked Gram.

"After the judging each booth gives away the dolls and characters. It is good luck to have one of them on your table for your Christmas feast. But soon they dry up and must be thrown away."

"All that work and they only last a few days!" said Gram, shaking her head.

"But of course," said Bernardo. "It is for the joy of doing it, of participating, and for the prize, if you win."

The men's fingers were nimble and I was amazed they didn't cut themselves. They twisted and turned the radishes as if they were on spools, making impressions that often left the radish with a face or a remarkable feature, like an elephant's knee in a knotty whorl. Outside the radishes were dark and brownish red. As the men scraped off the layers of skin, they revealed true red, the palest pinks, and in the heart of the radish, white. But the white was tainted, as if someone had tried to bleach a pink blouse, and around the edges of the seams, the faintest trace of rosy color remained.

I watched the men make magic out of vegetable and

copied them. The radishes cut like potatoes, only firmer, and gave way much easier than soap, which meant I made more mistakes. Beni said I could carve anything I liked, as long as it was an animal. I made little elephants, doves, bears, and squirrels, sticking at first to things I'd carved before.

At the end of the day, we covered the radishes with damp towels and set them in coolers.

The next day it was the same. We worked for hours, laughing and talking and singing songs in Spanish. I didn't even care that I didn't know all the words. Fabiola, Gram, and Flora made food and lemonade, and when Owen and Rubén's excitement could not be contained, Graciela took them away to find lucky spiders.

On the last day of carving, Beni brought in a radish that looked like a giant bulb.

"What will you do with that?" I asked.

"It is for the crown. The lion. We want you to carve it . . . to thank you for your idea."

I looked at Pedro and Bernardo and they nodded. I

took the radish from Beni, knowing that this was an honor. I held it up and examined it.

"The lion could be sitting, facing us, with the front legs straight and resting on its back legs. That way, I could carve the entire mane in a giant jagged circle."

"Yes," said Beni. *"Perfecto."*

I studied the radish again and made a few careful cuts. If I scraped a very thin layer of red in a long line, it curled slightly. Could I get a curly mane on *el león?* León. Thinking the name reminded me of the tiny thread of hope to which I clung. If my father came to the festival, would he see the radish tree full of animals and remember what he'd carved for us all those years ago? Would it make him happy? Would he like to know that his daughter was a carver, too?

"Today's the day," I whispered to Gram on the morning of the Night of the Radishes, waking her from a sound sleep. I had already dressed in my peasant blouse, jeans, and huaraches.

Gram sat up and pulled the light blanket around herself. "Naomi, what time is it?"

"Early, but I couldn't sleep."

Gram ran her hands through her thin hair and cleared her throat. "There's something I want to say to you before you get going."

I sat down next to her. "Gram, everything will be fine."

"Now let me talk. Lately . . . practical matters seem to be closing in on me."

"Like what?"

"Skyla might be right about a judge not wanting to separate a natural mother and her child, even after all the bad she's done. While I've been here, I have come to the conclusion that maybe I should be preparing you for that situation . . . just on the slim notion it might happen. I don't know how I would ever get along without you, but I'm more concerned with how you would get on without Owen and me."

"But it will not come to that," I said firmly. "Let's just plant that in our brains."

Gram laughed. "I am pleased you have adopted my positive attitudes, but even if we do find your father, I'm just not sure what kind of cake this mess will turn out to be. What if he wants you and Owen for himself? What if he wants you children to stay here with him? Then what?"

"Then you'll have to stay with us," I said, kissing her on the cheek. "And you'll have to learn some more Spanish."

After lunch, with Pedro, Bernardo, and Beni in the front seat and Owen, Rubén, and me crowded into the back, we rode in the truck to the center of Oaxaca City. Behind us in the truck bed, the coolers held the mysterious radishes. We unloaded the coolers and tubs of supplies on a corner, and Bernardo drove the truck back to Barrio Jalatlaco. He would walk the thirteen blocks back to the town square with the women.

We looked like a caravan of horses plowing through a field of tourists, our arms full of supplies: coolers, a metal washtub filled with radish leaves, bags with extra knives for last-minute tweaks, a big plastic bowl filled with moss, which we could use as a carpet for the scene. After finding our assigned table, the boys and I waited while the men checked in with the officials.

El zócalo was a square park bordered with large trees. Corralled in fancy black-iron fences, their wide branches created deep shade. In the middle of the park a fountain bubbled, and manicured hedges protected the flowerbeds dotted with blooms: yellow, red, orange, and white, like the rainbow of colors in the fruit vendor's stall at *el mercado.*

Next to the street, long tables had been set up for the festivities, surrounding the entire park for a block in each direction. In front of the tables a raised wooden viewing platform ran alongside, with a metal railing to keep those Gram called "the lookie-loos" a reasonable distance back. Like a frame inside a frame inside a frame, the trees, tables, and viewing platforms boxed the entire park, with openings now and then through which people could pass.

El zócalo blazed with colorful paper flags and giant balloon bouquets.

I looked at every man who passed on the street. Our father could be any of them. He could even be a man pretending to be our father and I wouldn't know the difference. Would I?

Beni, Pedro, and I spread the moss on the table. Owen and Rubén took their posts with the water bottles, waiting to spray something, anything. It wasn't long before Graciela, Flora, Fabiola, Gram, and Bernardo arrived.

I looked up at Bernardo. "I want to stay and help set up."

"It is more important that you are with Fabiola and the others to ask about your father," said Bernardo. "All of the carving is done. I promise we will make it look beautiful, and then you will be surprised like all the other *turistas*. There is much for you to see, as well."

The judging wasn't until five o'clock so we had time to start at the stall next to ours and walk slowly on the viewing platform around the entire park, along with hundreds of other people. The carvers added their final touches to their scenes and began to put out their secret best that they had held back until the last minute.

"I just can't believe that every detail of every figure has been made from a radish or some part of it," said Gram.

"It is true," said Fabiola. "It is forbidden to use anything else. One year someone used a carrot to carve a figure, for color, and they were eliminated from the competition."

I could hear the comments of the tourists as they stood near us.

"Remarkable."

"Magnificent."

"Unbelievable."

And it was all those things. Dolls dressed in elaborate gowns, musicians with trumpets, Nativity scenes with Mary, Joseph, and baby Jesus plus the sheep and camels and wise men. Bandits riding wild, rearing horses. Tall angels holding harps. Christ dying on a cross. School buses with children waving from the windows. A five-foot cathedral with the saints carved into the walls, just like the giant cathedral nearby. All made from giant radishes.

Fabiola or Graciela asked at each booth about our father. They found many who knew him well, but none who had seen him recently.

With every person who shook their head, Gram's face nodded politely, as if to say, "That's okay." But her eyes were telling me a different story. As we slowly inched closer to our own booth, I took Gram's hand and squeezed it.

She looked at me, downhearted. "We're running out of time, Naomi."

17 an exaltation of starlings

"Look!" said Graciela. "Everyone is crowding around our table."

It was true. We were almost back to our starting point, but we could hardly nudge our way to the front.

One lady even turned around and said, "Wait your turn."

I could see Bernardo, Pedro, and Beni's heads through the crowd, nodding and smiling.

Finally several people near the table moved, and I slipped through to the railing.

I had seen the individual pieces, but I never could have imagined how it all connected. Radish upon radish upon radish had been bound together with thin roots to create the giant trunk and sprawling branches. Radish leaves burst from the top. Fish of every size and shape appeared to swim up the trunk. Panthers prowled across a limb. Crocodiles and lizards lounged on the lower branches. A tiny row of elephants walked tails in trunks above them.

Deer and sheep and cows snuggled together in the saddles where the branches met. Beetles and butterflies attached to the leaves. Tiny birds poked through holes, their beaks open as if they were singing. And at the very top, my lion, the mane like a majestic sunburst.

The Complete and Unabridged Animal Kingdom with over 200 Photographs had come to roost in our tree.

"*¡Ay, qué hermoso!*" said Flora.

"Yes, beautiful," said Fabiola.

"It looks as if Noah chose this tree instead of an ark," said Gram.

Rubén and Owen gave an occasional dramatic squirt from their water bottles to keep the radishes moist.

"The judges, they are coming. Make room for them," said Fabiola.

We moved off to one side as a group of men and women with clipboards studied the presentation and made important marks on their papers. Soon they moved to the next stall farther down, and the entire crowd shifted with them.

"Now what?" I asked.

"We relax," said Beni. "We have fun at the festival. It is a big party, no? We give away some of the figures to people who admire them. And we wait for the announcements."

The band concert lasted until well after dark, and then came the results of the judging. We all crowded together. A man at a microphone began announcing the different categories. The first was *categoría tradicional,* meaning Nativities, cathedrals, and religious carvings. The speaker called the names for third, second, and first place, followed by cheers and applause from the crowd.

We waited through four more announcements.

Fabiola translated. "Next is our division, *categoría libre,* Free Design, meaning carvings of any imagination. This year the carvings have been extraordinary and compelling. Starting with third place . . . and receiving a cash award . . . and a commemorative certificate . . . are the Pérez brothers."

We clapped politely and knew exactly where the Pérez brothers were standing due to the rousing shouts on the other side of *el zócalo.*

"And in second place . . . and receiving a cash award and a commemorative certificate . . ." continued Fabiola, but she didn't need to continue because we heard the names.

"Bernardo Morales, Beni Morales, and Pedro Martínez!"

"Second place!" squealed Graciela. "We have never, ever been so honored!"

The men raised their arms in the air, jumped up and down, and clapped one another on the back, and we all cheered as loud as the Pérez brothers. Beni picked me up and swirled me around, and when Pedro and Bernardo hugged me, I laughed. We heard the results for first place, but it didn't matter. Gram got a bee in her bonnet because she thought the winner didn't hold a candle to our entry. Fabiola reassured her that there were always politics involved and that second place was *magnifico*.

Fireworks filled the sky with bright bursting spirals. After watching them, we all walked slowly toward the corner of *el zócalo*.

"Bernardo," called a voice. We all turned around. "I

heard your name. . . ." A man stood in front of us wearing white sports shoes and a red baseball cap.

Bernardo's face lit up. He opened his mouth to say something but before he could, the man looked from Bernardo to Gram to Owen to me. He seemed startled. Suddenly he turned and ran into the crowd.

I looked at Gram.

"It was him, Naomi," she said, her eyes still looking in the direction he had run.

Before I knew it, I was running after him, following the red cap as it bobbed through the crowds. I heard Owen calling my name behind me. I dodged a hive of tourists. I bumped into a man selling balloons. *"Perdóneme,"* I said, watching the red cap. Another man held out a plastic sandwich bag in front of me, filled with cucumbers salted with red pepper. I pushed his arm aside. I could see the red cap up ahead, going toward the square in front of the cathedral. I skirted blankets displaying hundreds of *alebrijes,* ran through rows of tents selling rugs and shawls, black pottery, painted plates, knives, and leather purses. I followed the red baseball cap all the way to the corner where a woman sat under an umbrella selling fried grasshoppers. Then the cap disappeared down a side street jammed with stalls. He never looked back, not once.

I stopped, breathing heavily. Why had he run? I had wanted to yell out to him, but what would I call him? Father? Santiago? I turned in a circle for one last look around. The band began to play a loud march in the gazebo in the middle of the park. The colors and sounds blurred as if the world was spinning. When it all stopped, I was alone with the fried grasshopper lady.

"Naomi Outlaw, you scared me to death running off like that," said Gram when I worked my way back to her. "Don't you ever do that again!"

"I . . . I didn't want him to get away. Where did he go? Why didn't he stay?" Every question that came to my mind seemed to put me into a deeper stew of confusion.

Graciela tried to calm me down. "He was surprised. That is all. I am sure he does not know why you are here.

He could be frightened that you think bad of him for not coming back to get you when you were a little girl. We know now he is in town, and we can call your aunt Teresa in the morning."

"What if he didn't go to Aunt Teresa's? What if he ran away for good?" I said.

"There is nothing to be done tonight. Tomorrow, okay?" said Graciela, reaching out for my hand.

As we passed in front of the cathedral, Rubén ran ahead and Owen followed. We caught up with them in front of a street vendor selling *buñuelos,* fried tortillas with a syrupy glaze, served in a shallow terra-cotta bowl. Bernardo bought one for each of us, and we sat on the curb, eating the crunchy sweet.

But I could hardly eat. I only finished half and asked Graciela where I should put the bowl.

"You must throw your bowl in the courtyard near the side of the church. Look. Over there."

We turned to see a man and a woman facing away from the church and throwing their bowls back over their shoulders toward a courtyard The bowls shattered on the cobblestones and landed among thousands of pottery pieces.

"It is tradition so that good luck will follow you into the New Year," said Fabiola. "You must do the same."

"Well, we could use a little more luck," said Gram. "And I know it will be right up Owen's alley. Come on, everybody."

I hesitated.

"Naomi, come on," called Owen, his eyes pleading.

I got up and followed them to the spot on the street. We flung our bowls, like brides tossing bouquets, then turned to see them break in a shower of clattering shards. Owen rocked around in a crooked circle and Rubén jumped up and down, clapping and cheering.

"See, Naomi," said Owen. "Now, we'll be lucky."

I was too worn out to argue.

We finally started home to Barrio Jalatlaco, except for the men who were headed off to celebrate their victory. Owen and Rubén pleaded to go with them, but Gram said it was no place for young boys. Before we separated, Bernardo handed me a small shopping bag. "The lion, Naomi. It's for you. Spray it as soon as you get home."

I smiled and took it from him, knowing he was trying to cheer me.

As we walked through the streets carrying the empty coolers, the sounds of the festival quieted behind us. The talk was about the contest. Graciela told us that the entire barrio would talk of nothing else for months.

As we turned down our street, we heard the distant barking of a frantic dog.

"That's Lulu," said Owen.

"*Los vecinos*," said Flora, shaking her head and clicking her tongue.

"The poor neighbors," said Fabiola. "I hope she did not bark all night. Sometimes she does not like to be left alone."

We hurried down the block and into the yard, lit only by the moon. Flora struggled to unlock the door, to release the whining Lulu, but before she could get it open, suddenly the jacaranda tree rustled, startling us. We all turned toward it, but it was just a spray of blossoms sprinkling down. Something didn't seem right, though, and a shiver raced up my spine. As the last jacaranda bloom drifted to the ground, I realized there wasn't a whisper of wind.

18   a pride of lions

A figure stepped out of the shadows.

Gram put her hand on her heart. Fabiola instinctively pulled me close to her.

"Who's there?!" demanded Graciela.

"It . . . it is me . . . Santiago."

"Gracias a Diós," said Flora, making the sign of the cross and hurrying into the house to turn on the porch light, which flooded the yard.

Gram and Fabiola reached Santiago first. Gram grabbed both of his hands and said, "Santiago, we've been looking for you!" He hung his head and said something that I couldn't hear, and Gram shook her head and said, "No, no . . . don't say that. We're just happy we found you." Then she hugged him.

I froze. I might as well have been back on the playground with a bunch of kids calling Owen names and me watching it all like a movie. Was this really happening?

Owen ran forward. Santiago put his hands on Owen's

arms. I could hear bits and pieces of Owen's nonstop jabbering.

". . . looking and looking for you. . . . It took a long, long time in Baby Beluga . . . to Mexico . . . and Barrio Jalatlaco . . ."

Santiago touched Owen's head and stroked his hair.

What did that feel like?

Owen wouldn't stop talking. ". . . and we came with Bernardo and Fabiola and Lulu. . . . Rubén is my best friend. . . . firecrackers and candy . . . Naomi ran after you. . . . thought you were lost. . . ."

When Owen said my name, Santiago looked up. His forehead wrinkled, and he ran a hand through his rumpled brown hair. He swallowed, and I saw the gulp ride down his throat. He reached an arm toward me.

Graciela took the bag from my hand and gently tried to push me forward.

I wanted to go to him but I felt as if I was knee-deep in wet cement. I opened my mouth to say something, anything, but only tears came out.

Santiago scooped Owen up with one arm and walked to me. Then he knelt down on one knee, reached out, and pulled me into his arms. At first he rocked us back and forth like people do when they're just plain happy to see a friend, but then he became still and pulled us even closer. I knew he was crying by the way his chest was sputtering up and down and by the sounds of his sniffling. I clung on tight to him and he squeezed back over and over, his arms strong and protective. When I pressed my face into his shirt, I smelled sea salt and . . . was I dreaming? A whiff of soap.

"*Mis niños. Mis niños,*" he said, burying his face in our hair.

When we stood up, there wasn't a dry eye in heaven. Fabiola started talking in Spanish and introduced everyone. We all went inside and, even though it was late, we crowded around the kitchen table.

"We look for you," said Rubén.

"I did not arrive until tonight," explained Santiago, reaching over and ruffling Rubén's hair. "My car was not working and I had to take a bus, but the drivers are on strike so I waited in the bus station for three days. I knew I would not arrive in time to carve in the festival. For that, I was very sad. I almost did not come, but something . . . something told me I must come."

"It was all of our positive thinking," I said quietly.

"Yes, maybe," said Santiago, smiling. "I went straight to *el zócalo* to hear the announcements and when I heard Bernardo's name, I could not believe it. I went to find him and then, when I saw María and Naomi and Owen . . . I wondered if it could be true. My children? But I wanted to think, to prepare . . . so I ran."

"I chased you," I said.

"I did not know. I took a taxi to the house of Teresa. She told me you came to see her and where you were staying. Then I could not stop thinking about you. I knew I had to come." Santiago seemed shy, but maybe that was because we had all seen him crying earlier, or maybe he was just quiet, like me.

I related the whole story of what happened and how we got here, with a little help from Graciela because

Santiago's English wasn't what it used to be. I sat beside him and as he listened and nodded with a sad, tired face, he reached down and stroked my hair.

"Tell us what you have been doing," said Fabiola.

Santiago shrugged his shoulders. "I have lived in Puerto Escondido for the last seven years. I have a boat and I take the tourists out to catch fish. It is a small living. And the town, it is becoming more popular now, especially to the surfers. I don't make the big money like I made in the United States, but it is very cheap to live there. I have a little house, and when I am not working on the boat, I carve the animals. I bring them to Aunt Teresa and she paints them. They are sold in some shops. I sometimes make more money from the carvings than from the fishing." He looked at me and Owen. A tiny smile showed on his face. "Do you want to know the name of my boat? It is the *Soledad,* after my children."

"Soledad is the saint, right?" I said.

"That is right. You were named for *Nuestra Señora de la Soledad.* But my boat was named for you."

"Santiago, there are some things I'd like to talk to you about. Maybe tomorrow? We need some help," said Gram.

He sat forward, leaning his elbows on his knees and resting his chin on his folded hands. Looking at me and then Owen, he said to Gram, "I have thought of nothing else for years."

I looked around at everyone sitting in Flora's kitchen and I felt as if I were in a movie, in a scene that was crystal clear in the middle and soft and blurry around the edges. I didn't want it to end. I only wanted to be right here, right now. I wanted to remember everything about this night.

Graciela took Owen and Rubén to get ready for bed, and the late hour soon settled on everyone. Santiago stood up to leave.

"Wait," I said, reaching for the bag on the table and bringing out the lion.

I handed it to Santiago. "For you."

Santiago looked at the lion, but a sadness overtook his face. He shook his head back and forth. "It is the first year that a León did not carve in the contest."

Fabiola smiled. "But you are wrong. A León did carve in the contest. Naomi, she did this."

Puzzled, Santiago looked at me, then at the lion. He examined it carefully, turning it around and touching the nicks and cuts. "It is *fantástico!*"

Even after I was in Baby Beluga and snug in my bed, I could still see the pride in my father's eyes when he had admired the lion. The occasional pop of a firecracker kept me awake to revel in my thoughts. I was in my own bed. Gram and Owen were here with me. Everything was the same. Well, almost everything. Rubén was sleeping inside Baby Beluga, too. We were now in Mexico. I had found my father. And a waterfall of happiness had drowned my nagging worries, at least for now.

First thing in the morning, I would make *fantástico* number one on my "Superb Spanish Words" list.

19 a cry of hounds

On Christmas morning Owen and I stood in the yard and looked up. I had to pinch myself to make sure I was not dreaming. A jungle of painted beasts floated beneath the jacaranda tree, the leaves and purple flowers like a canopy above them. Tied to the branches with transparent fishing line, the carved wooden animals appeared suspended. When a warm breeze tickled the dragons, reptiles, birds, and lions, they twirled and swayed.

Owen and I lay down on the ground and watched them. A few minutes later Santiago came out from behind the trailer, where he had been waiting. He lay down next to us and we watched the spectacle to the music of Owen's raspy laughter.

Later in the afternoon I sat outside, carving with Santiago. He was an expert on wood and had brought some of the special copal branches from the trees in the mountains. I loved watching him carve.

He held up a curved branch. "Each piece has a personality. Sometimes you can look at the wood and see exactly what it might be. The promise reveals itself early. Other times you must let your imagination dictate what you will find. How do you see your soap today? It is a dog, right?"

I nodded. I had been working on it for several days. "This end will be the tail. And here" — I pointed to the bottom corner — "will be one of its legs, running."

Santiago nodded.

Almost done, I pulled my knife across the soap but dug a little too deep and a large piece crumbled to the ground. With one slip of the knife, I had accidentally carved off the running leg.

I gasped.

"No, do not be sad," said Santiago. "There is still some magic left inside. Let us say that the missing leg is *simbólico* of a tragedy or something the dog has lost. Or that its destiny was to be a dog with three legs." He picked up my carving, and with a few strokes of the knife smoothed the ragged piece into a perfect three-legged dog. "You must carve so that what is inside can become what it is meant to be. When you are finished, the magic will show itself for what it really is."

Santiago considered an odd-shaped piece of wood. "When the promise does not reveal itself early, your imagination must dictate your intentions. Then the wood, or the soap, it will become what you least expect. Sometimes the wood fools me. I think I am carving a parrot, and when I am finished it has a fish tail. Or I begin a tiger, and in the end it has the body of a dancer."

With the small machete, he scraped at the layers of bark that had built up over time, exposing the innards of what used to be a tree branch and revealing the unprotected heart meat. He traded the machete for a knife and chaffed at the wood with quick strokes. Soon he handed me a rough figure.

I held it up in the air. I could see that it was a lion's body with a human's head, maybe that of a girl.

As I turned it around, admiring it, Gram came out of

the house and slowly sat down in one of the chairs. She stared at her folded hands and cleared her throat. "I just checked in with Mrs. Maloney. The mediator, a young woman, showed up at Avocado Acres yesterday to interview her. Imagine showing up on Christmas Eve! The woman asked Mrs. Maloney where we were because she needs to talk to all of us by Friday, January third. Mrs. Maloney told her we'd return from our family vacation in time for the interview, which is what I had told her to say if anybody asked. That's in nine days, and what with four or five days' driving ahead of us . . . I'm sorry, Naomi, but Bernardo said we should leave the day after tomorrow."

I took a deep breath and looked around the yard. "Can't we just stay here?" I asked, my hands suddenly quivering. "You like it here. You said so yourself." I heard Owen's and Rubén's giggles coming from the garden. "Owen loves it and we could . . . we could go to school here. We're learning Spanish real good. Or . . . or we could go to Puerto Escondido and live in the little house and help sell the carvings. . . . I could learn to paint them, like Aunt Teresa . . . and . . ."

Santiago pulled me from my chair to his side on a small wooden bench. He put his arm around me.

"Naomi, I would love for you to come to my house, but right now your life is in California. I have written the letter for the judge. I told the truth about your mother and that my wishes are for you and Owen to live with María. I told that I want to be a part of your life and see you . . . maybe in the summer for vacations if that is all right with you and Owen. More, if it is possible."

My lips trembled. I stared at the ground.

"I did not fight for you when you were little," said Santiago. "It is something for which I am sorry. I should not have believed your mother when she said I would never be able to see you. If I had been stronger, maybe things could have been different, but maybe they would not have been so different. . . . How will we ever know?"

I looked at him. "But why can't you come with us?"

"For that to happen," he said, "I would have to prepare. Much would need to be done. Sell my house. My boat. Much of my money comes from my carvings, which are sold only in Oaxaca. My work, it is here."

"But what if the judge —"

"Naomi," said Gram, "we are not going to consider the worst that could happen. Thinking that way does not help self-prophecies."

Since we'd found Santiago, Gram was wearing her fierceness again. At least on the outside.

"I guess I better tell Owen," said Gram.

"I will go with you," said Santiago, and they headed toward the garden.

Alone, beneath the jacaranda, I stared at the three-legged dog and the lion girl in my lap.

We rode home to Lemon Tree silently. The truck and Baby Beluga seemed to drag along the highway. We traveled with less than we had brought, choosing to leave many things for Flora, Pedro, Graciela, and Rubén. So why did we seem to plod along? Did the weight of our memories slow us down?

For hundreds of kilometers, I held the lion girl and thought about all that I wanted to tell Blanca, especially about my father.

On our last days in Oaxaca, Owen and I had gone everywhere with Santiago: to visit Aunt Teresa, to *el zócalo,* to *el mercado* for pineapple-coconut ice cream. And to admire the statue of Soledad in *la basílica.*

I would never forget that day. The statue with the long robe, a crown of gold, the sparkling stained-glass windows. Our footsteps echoing on the floor. Holding Santiago's hand and listening to his adoration.

"*Our Lady of Solitude* is loved by sailors and fishermen," he said. "She protects us at sea: when our boats are rocking in a storm, when it is foggy and we cannot see the way, when we need to get home and our motor fails us. Then we ask for her assistance. She is part of Oaxaca. And since you have her name and have been here to see the wonder of this city, Oaxaca is part of you."

The morning we left, Santiago came early to help Bernardo load the last of the luggage. He cut down all the animals hanging from the jacaranda and gave them to Owen and me.

It was a long good-bye, what with Flora running back and forth to the kitchen with one more bundle of tamales and Pedro rechecking the tires on the truck and the trailer. And Graciela and Beni chasing Owen, Rubén, and Lulu around the yard. It was the kind of good-bye where everyone hugged and kissed every single person, then stood around talking and looking at each other, then all of a sudden started hugging and kissing everyone again, crying a little each time.

When we were finally ready to climb into the truck, Santiago hugged me and said, "Be brave, Naomi León."

I nodded, but when he took me in his arms one more time and rocked me back and forth, I didn't pretend to be brave.

"Do not be sad," he whispered. "We have found each other. I will write. You will write. We have much for which to be thankful and everything will be the way it was meant to be. You will see. I promise. I promise. Now you must promise."

"I promise."

The truck jolted as Bernardo downshifted on the highway. Oaxaca had long disappeared from our view. I opened my notebook to make a list of all that I hoped to remember, but I closed it. My pen seemed too heavy to lift.

20 a crash of hippopotami

The day before school started, we arrived at the courthouse too early, which didn't help my jitters. Gram,
Owen, and I waited on a bench outside our assigned room.
The mediator lady had come to Lemon Tree on Friday, just
as planned, wearing a suit and hugging her clipboard. She
had been nice, but all business, asking Owen and me each
privately about a million questions, like: What did Gram
feed us? How many times a week did we take a bath?
Had we ever contracted head lice? Now, sitting in the
courthouse and staring down the long hallway with the
perfectly shined floors, I hoped I had answered correctly.

There was no sign of Skyla or Clive.

A man approached Gram. "Are you Mary Outlaw?"

"Yes, sir," she said.

"I'm the clerk. Right this way. The judge will be here
in a few minutes." He opened the door and held it while
we walked inside.

The courtroom did not look like the ones on television

with the wood railings and oak chairs and a tall box for the witness. It was a small room with a desk at the front. Built-in seats, like the kind at the movies, were arranged in three short rows. One lone seat was positioned next to the judge's desk.

I looked around the room. Posters of children hung on the walls: teenagers playing basketball, a little boy and girl hugging a very old lady, children sliding down slides with their hands in the air, and a circle of babies in cute outfits. I guessed it was like those friendly rooms at Children's Hospital. The court wanted the room to feel not so scary when they gave you the bad news.

Skyla walked in at the last minute with Clive, but at first I wasn't sure it was either one of them. Skyla wore a pale-pink skirt and sweater set, nylons, flat pink slip-on shoes, and a strand of pearls. Her hair was natural-looking light brown and she wore hardly a lick of makeup, except for a bubble-gum pink lipstick. Clive's hair had been buzzed short, as if he was enlisting in the military. He wore slacks and a shirt with a button-down collar.

Gram leaned in to me. "Well, don't they look like the all-American couple." I didn't know if Gram was trying to make a joke or if she was as scared as I was.

When Skyla saw me and Owen, she waved at us as if nothing was wrong. As if she wasn't trying to do something horrible and mean to our family.

"I have missed you so much!" she said from across the room. Her voice was so sugar-coated that I wondered who the show was for. The only other person in the room was the clerk, and he wasn't paying a nickel of attention.

The judge came in and sat down and we did the same. Skyla and Clive on one side and Gram, Owen, and I on the other. Even though the judge looked friendly with smile wrinkles around her eyes like Fabiola's, as soon as I saw that black robe, I shuddered inside. It meant the law, that whatever the judge said would have to be carried out.

"Let's get started," she said. "Ms. Skyla Jones, I'll hear from you first. I see here that you left Naomi and Owen in the care of your grandmother seven years ago."

Skyla stood. "Yes, your honor, I did leave them with my grandmother after some rather awful circumstances."

"And what were those?"

"I was getting out of a bad marriage. I didn't have any money and I needed time to make a life for myself . . . and my children."

"So this separation was not something you wanted?"

"Oh, no! No mother *wants* to be apart from her children." Skyla glanced over at us. She looked like an angel.

Gram took my hand.

"Ms. Jones, can you explain what you've been doing during the past seven years?"

"I have had some trouble, your honor, but that has all changed. I admit I have been in rehabilitation but I have recently been successful in completing a" — she looked at Clive — "a comprehensive program."

Clive nodded and smiled at Skyla.

"There are doctors' reports here about alcohol-induced mental illness," said the judge. "Were you going to leave that out?"

"No, of course not. I am on medication and I have not missed one dose. And part of my rehabilitation is to establish a relationship with my children. More than anything, that is what I want." Skyla looked lovingly toward us.

"I applaud your efforts, Ms. Jones," said the judge. "You may sit down."

I bit my lip. If Skyla had acted like this when she was interviewed, what had been the mediator's recommendation to the judge?

"Mrs. Outlaw?" said the judge.

Gram stood up. "Yes, ma'am."

"How old are you?"

"I am sixty-nine years old."

"And you are in good health?"

"Yes, very," said Gram.

The judge's voice softened. "But the reality is clear, isn't it? You are not a young woman."

"Yes, ma'am, that's true, but I take good care of myself and if something happens to me, their father, Santiago León, will step forward and help. He wants the children to stay with me and he hopes to visit them as much as possible. He wrote a letter saying as much."

When they heard our father's name, Skyla and Clive put their heads together and started whispering.

The judge raised her eyebrows and looked through the file in front of her. "Let's see . . . I have here notarized letters from a Ms. Morimoto, a Mr. Marble, both teachers at the children's school, commending you for your dedication to Naomi and Owen. I have a similar letter from a Mrs. Maloney, a neighbor, and reports from Naomi's counselor and two doctors at Children's Hospital. And . . ." The judge put one paper in front of the others and studied it. "Here it is . . . a notarized letter from the children's father. It says he was discouraged from trying to contact the children by Ms. Jones but has continued to send financial assistance and now wants to establish a visitation schedule to maintain his relationship with them."

"That's right," said Gram.

"Ms. Jones, what do you have to say about this?"

Skyla looked at Clive and nodded, then faced the judge. "I was very young and immature when I left the children with my grandmother. I regret many of my actions during that time of my life."

"And you would be fine with a visitation schedule for your ex-husband."

"Oh, yes, your honor. I only want what's best. That's what I told the woman the other day when she interviewed me. That's why Naomi, especially, needs to be with me. She needs her mother, not a great-grandmother, who is so far removed from the . . . from the . . . contemporary issues of her life."

"That's very good, Ms. Jones." The judge gave Skyla a peculiar smile, then looked back at the papers in her hand. "I have the recommendation of the mediator before me, but before I make the final decision, I would like to hear from the children. Naomi, would you come up here, please?"

I stood up and looked at Gram. She patted my arm and

pointed to the chair next to the judge's desk. I walked over and sat down, facing directly across from Skyla. I couldn't take my eyes off the perfect *M* of her lips.

"Naomi?" The judge's voice finally got my attention. "Look at me, please."

I turned toward the black robe.

"I need to explain something. I am always very hesitant to separate parents and children. I feel they should be together whenever possible, except for unusual circumstances. As long as your mother refrains from alcohol and takes her medications and has a good-faith intention of caring for you, I could not, with any good conscience, deny your mother her parental rights, unless I heard a compelling reason. So can you give me any reason why you *shouldn't* be with your mother?"

I heard the judge's words, but I couldn't believe them. I was going to have to live with Skyla.

I wanted to tell the judge everything. I wanted to say that I needed to live with Gram and Owen because I didn't know my mother very well and that she scared me. My mind said the words, but my mouth couldn't form them. With everyone staring at me, a brick wall had sprouted between my words and the world, without a crack of daylight for a whisper to escape.

"Naomi, if you can't add any different information to this situation . . ."

Skyla sat up straight, wiggled in her seat, and squeezed Clive's arm.

I closed my eyes and heard my father's words, "Be brave, Naomi León."

I felt a rumbling in my mind, the sound a bulldozer makes when it is headed toward you. A sensation came over me, as if someone had unlatched a gate that freed a herd of lunging wild animals. I opened my eyes to find Skyla's gaze drilling into me.

"Is that what you want, Naomi? To live with your mother?" asked the judge.

I looked at Gram and Owen, and slowly shook my head. "No," I said.

"A little louder, Naomi. I can't hear you."

It was as if the stampede crashed through the wall in front of me. "No," I said again, and slowly began telling the story from the beginning. How Gram was a widow and lost her only daughter. How Skyla and Santiago got married and took us to Mexico and Skyla gave us to Gram so she could find her life. How Santiago loved us, but Skyla wouldn't let him have us. How we lived at Avocado Acres next to the avocado grove in Lemon Tree so Owen could have room to be a wild monkey.

I kept talking, louder now. "Gram loves us and takes care of us. She's been both our parents all rolled into one, until we met our father. Lemon Tree is my home. That's where I belong. I don't want to go to Las Vegas to live with Skyla. Skyla said she would hurt Gram. She said something *bad* might happen to Gram if I didn't go with her to Las Vegas."

As if a dam had burst, I couldn't stop the rush of words. I told how Skyla just wanted me to be a baby-sitter for Sapphire and how she had started drinking again and about the slap and how there was more where that came from. I said I loved my school and my friend, Blanca. I told about my carvings and Children's Hospital and Owen being an FLK and how Skyla didn't want him anymore because she thought he was a Blem. Then I told about my father and how we had found him. I told the judge about self-prophecy and how if you wanted something to happen you should say it was going to happen over and over again and how I had been thinking "Everything will be all right. I'll always be with Gram and Owen" at least a million times since Mexico.

I said all that with Skyla and Clive looking right at me.

Skyla stood up. "Your honor, she has always had an overactive imagination. I need my little girl and she needs me. We belong together, just Naomi and me. Can't you see that what she's been telling you is just little white lies?" Skyla sat down and started weeping and blotting her eyes with a tissue. I swore she was making her eyes red on purpose by pressing too hard.

I turned to the judge and said in a very strong voice, "I am not lying."

"Thank you, Naomi," said the judge. "You may sit down."

The judge looked confused. "Ms. Jones, there's one issue I need clarified before I can rule. Do I understand correctly that you only want Naomi?"

Skyla immediately composed herself. "Yes. That's all I want, your honor. My daughter."

"And why don't you want your son?"

"Well, that's not the issue. I'm Naomi's mother and I have a right —"

"Ms. Jones, I will decide the issue. Now, why don't you want your son?"

Skyla seemed flustered and looked at Clive. "Well . . . when he was born . . . he had so many *problems* that I never really *connected* with him . . . bonded with him. I only had him one year of his life so he doesn't even remember me, and I really don't remember much about him. Naomi being older and a girl and all, we're more suited in a mother-daughter way, if you know what I mean."

"So you have no intention of taking both of the children away from Mrs. Outlaw," said the judge.

"Oh, no, your honor."

"Ms. Jones, did you relay this information to the mediator during the interview?"

"Well, no, I figured that was my own personal choice. See, Owen's better off in Lemon Tree and Naomi's better off with me. We should be together," said Skyla, smiling, and obviously satisfied with her answer.

I looked at Owen, who was on the other side of Gram. Gram had her arm around him and he did not look sad or anything. If he found Skyla's words upsetting, there was enough tape plastered across his shirt to hold him together.

"Well then," said the judge. "I don't need to take additional time to consider this case. I am ready to rule. I rarely withhold parental rights and the mediator did recommend that the children live with their mother. But I believe she did not understand the issue in its entirety, especially since Ms. Jones was not forthcoming. I am extremely hesitant to separate siblings who have lived together their entire lives. That is something I will *not* do, especially when there are loving, attentive, and responsible relatives to act as their caregivers, such as Mrs. Outlaw and the father, who both clearly want these children. Since Ms. Jones has established her preference to this court, which is clearly not in the best interest of Naomi and Owen, I grant guardianship to Mrs. Outlaw. Ms. Jones, we can set up a supervised visitation schedule for you, if you like, to visit *both* of your children." The judge pounded the gavel. "This hearing is over."

Skyla looked confused. Clive grabbed her hand and they hurried out of the courtroom. He never looked back, but Skyla did. She raised her free hand and gave us a weak smile and a little wave of her fingers before Clive pulled her out the door.

"Let's go," said Gram, wrapping an arm around each of us.

She drove us toward home. We were almost to Avocado Acres when Gram turned right instead of left at the corner.

21 a brood of chicks

On Wednesday, the first day back to school after the break, Blanca was waiting on the steps for me. "Wow. I missed you," she said, hugging me tight. "I heard you went to Mexico. Tell me all about it! I'm full Mexican and I've never even been there, except for Tijuana, and that doesn't really count since it's practically in San Diego. Hey, your bangs are longer. You've only got two clips on each side. Big news. There's someone new at lunch in the library. His name is Midah Bakiano."

We laughed. Midah Bakiano was a shoo-in for my "Unusual Names" list. I told Blanca as much as I could about everything on our way to class.

Ms. Morimoto gave me a hug, too. "Naomi, finally! You're back. I was worried you wouldn't make it to the play this weekend. I'm so happy you'll be joining us."

At lunch, Mr. Marble said, "Naomi Outlaw! I'm ecstatic to see you!" (I added *ecstatic* to my "Splendid Words" list.) "Now we have our little nest of library chicks all back in their usual places," he said, counting and pointing at John Lee, Mimi Messmaker, Midah Bakiano, Blanca, and me. "All is right with the world."

After lunch, while Blanca visited with Midah Bakiano and talked his ear off, I got up the courage to show Mr. Marble some of my carvings. I pulled the figures, wrapped in paper towel, out of my backpack and arranged the families of reptiles, birds, tigers, and lions on the check-out counter. I lined up the ducklings and the fish and the elephants. And I told him how I had carved in *La Noche de los Rábanos*.

He said, "Naomi Outlaw, you are a girl of great talent and many layers. Who knew? Thank you for sharing these with me! I am overwhelmed with delight. Would you allow me to feature these in the glass case for Open House in a few months? I always save the spectacular collections for that event."

Would I allow him? To be in the glass case for Open House for the entire school and their families to see? It was the highest honor at Buena Vista Elementary. It could be my claim to fame.

The library lunch bunch crowded around.

"Wow, Naomi the Lion," said Blanca. "Those are amazing!"

"You carved those?" said Mimi Messmaker. "That looks hard."

I guessed that was the best I would get from Mimi but I didn't care.

Mr. Marble considered me in a thoughtful way. "I can already tell you are a different girl since you went to Mexico. Before you were a mouse, but now you have the countenance of a lioness."

I loved Mr. Marble.

After school Blanca waited on the steps with Owen and me, like always. When Gram pulled up in the Toyota, Blanca said, "Bye, Naomi the Lion. I'll see you in the morning, right here." She pointed to the steps.

"Bye," I called to her and waved.

She looked at me funny. "You know something, Naomi? Your voice is louder."

a murmuration of tomorrows

On the outside of things, nothing much had changed. Gram still made some of our clothes and we still lived in Baby Beluga at Avocado Acres in Lemon Tree. We went to Spray 'n Play to make sundaes and watch the cars go through the wash. My hair was still unruly, but it finally grew out to where I only needed one clip on each side to keep it back. Some days I wore it half up and half down, just like Graciela.

On the inside though, I was different. I had experienced Barrio Jalatlaco, Las Posadas, and quesillo. I had walked on cobblestone streets and thrown pottery at a church, just for the sake of good luck. Me!

I had discovered my mother. I supposed Owen and I would always long for her a little and wonder what it would have been like if she had been different. Gram said Skyla could clean up her act and try and take us back to court someday but that we shouldn't count those chickens before they hatched. Gram said it wasn't likely that Skyla would make the effort to visit us, either, but if she did, I wouldn't mind. I would like to feel her hands on my head, French braiding my hair again. It was funny how she was nice in a mean way, and mean in a nice way. There it was again, the good and bad all rolled into a meatball.

I had also found my father, who had loved me for a long time without being nearby. How many others were walking around and not even knowing that someone far away cared for them? Imagine all that love floating in the air, waiting to land on someone's life!

Although we had discovered our parents, our lives with Gram were carved into our beings. We were her prizes, and that was good enough for us.

Santiago had taught me that you must carve what your imagination dictates so that what is inside can become what it is meant to be. In the end, the figure will reveal itself for what it really is.

It was true. In Mexico, I had seen carvings of wooden angels with horns, a parrot with a fish tail, a lizard with wings, a three-legged dog. It worked the same with people, too.

A mother with a cat's claws.

A father with a lion's heart.

A great-grandmother with a bird's protective outstretched wings.

A mouse with a lioness's voice.

I might have begun with a whisper, but it had been strong enough to make a self-prophecy come true. I found a foot-stomping holler that would be loud enough to say boo to those boys someday. I could now overcome an army of worries. I even made a promise to our father—which I intended to keep—that no matter where we lived, we'd all travel to Oaxaca every year at Christmastime for the Night of the Radishes. After all, a León had been carving in the competition for over one hundred years.

I hoped my father was right, that like the figures we carved from wood and soap, I was becoming who I was meant to be, the Naomi Soledad León Outlaw of my wildest dreams.